Grace Logan and the Goblin Bones

by

Pam Binder

Grace Logan and the Goblin Bones

COPYRIGHT © 2018 by Pam Binder

Cover Art by *Kristian Norris*

The Wild Rose Press, Inc.
PO Box 708
Adams Basin, NY 14410-0708
Visit us at www.thewildrosepress.com

Publishing History
First Fantasy Rose Edition, 2018
Print ISBN 978-1-5092-2266-7
Digital ISBN 978-1-5092-2267-4

Published in the United States of America

Mac Tíre gave me an uneasy look. "What's with Grace?"

Síofra reached out toward me and gave my hand a gentle squeeze. "She's seeing our world for the first time. She's not prepared."

Mac Tíre's eyebrows knitted together and shook his head. "It's all happened too fast for her." He moved toward me and rested his hand on my shoulder. "Grace, you can take off the ring. You'll remember everything that has happened but at least you won't see goblins, or things like Finn's wings anymore, and we will hide you until this is over."

"Mac Tíre is right," Síofra said. "We are part of this, but you can choose."

I glanced down at the ring on my finger. Mac Tíre had given me a way out. I didn't have to get involved. It was one thing to dream of monsters and things that went bump in the night, another to know they existed. Talking it off seemed like good advice, but my mother had given me the ring. She believed in me. The next step was to believe in myself.

Praise for Pam Binder

"Pam Binder gracefully weaves elements of humor, magic and romantic tension."

~Publishers Weekly

~*~

Awards
2018 Romantic Times
Pioneers of Romance Fiction Award
for helping forge the way for the many subgenres
in romance

~

FALLING IN LOVE WITH EMMA
was a 2018 finalist in
the Desert Rose RWA Golden Quill Contest

Dedication

To our grandson, James Arman (Jimmy),
and his wonderful parents, Scott and Lydia.
May your life be filled with love, adventure,
and happily-ever-afters.

Chapter One

Ireland, sixteenth century

Word of my arranged marriage spread over our land faster than mice abandon a sinking ship. Warlords, chieftains, and curious land-owners from as far away as Galway poured into our castle. The only clans missing were the O'Briens. They, and my betrothed, would arrive on the day I turned fifteen, the eve of Samhain, one week from today.

Wearing the gown Mother had chosen for me for tonight's celebrations, I headed down the path along the cliffs that led to the shadows of the forest. An arranged marriage was the least of my worries. I was determined to find my best friend. If anyone knew the meaning of what I'd seen last night, it was Síofra.

I avoided the bonfires that ringed our castle like golden beads on the necklace of a fairy queen, their glow unnatural and cold as though they were enchanted. It was dusk, at summer's end, and the first day of the seven-day festival leading to Halloween. We Irish call this day All Hollow's Eve, or Samhain. This time of year, we were most afraid of the dark. The fact I'd heard a Banshee's wail last night and seen the image of the Dullahan, Ireland's Headless Horseman, race across the moon didn't help.

The Banshee is a herald of death and the Dullahan

captures the souls.

Father said every Irish clan of importance had a Banshee. We called ours Cally. He never talked much about the Dullahan.

My formal name is Granuaile Logan, but everyone calls me Grace. I am tall for my age, and Mother tells me that if I don't stop growing I'll tower over Father. I have green eyes and red, curly hair I tame into a single braid during sword practice or when I'm pretending I'm a pirate. But today I feel that my dream of sailing my own ship will never come.

The sky darkened over the jagged cliffs as though reflecting my thoughts.

The rock wall formed a natural barrier along the ocean side of our castle and discouraged attacks from the sea. I hesitated near the cliffs and stood on tip-toes to try and catch a glimpse of Father's ship, the *Red Branch*, named for a legendary army of Irish knights. Despite my pleas, Father refused to take me on his voyage. It was the first time I hadn't waved goodbye when his ship left the dock.

Generations of Logans had built their wealth by the motto "Fortune Favors the Bold." I doubted we were the only ones to live by those words, but my father took them seriously. Every step he took, every word he spoke, and every battle he fought, he weighed against our motto. Except, of course, when it came to his daughter. For a girl, being bold was a flaw, not a virtue.

A cat wailed out a protest.

I smiled. I'd recognize Ella's distress-meow anywhere. Directly below on a narrow ledge, Ella was tangled in a bluish-green Gorse shrub, bursting with prickly spikes. The more she struggled, the more the branches tightened around her.

The tips of her fur were the color of rust, as though she'd spent too much time bathing in the sun. She followed me around as though it was her personal duty to protect me, but it was a toss-up as to who was protecting whom. I'd rescued her from trees, and when my small boat tipped over, I'd pulled her out of the water. And she was the perfect watch-kitty, alerting me when my mother had hired a new tutor.

"Don't worry, little one, I'm here." I flopped down on my stomach, reached below, ignoring the scrapes across my hands, and disentangled her from the branches. If I didn't free her, she'd plummet to the rocks and sea below.

I scooped her up in my arms and nuzzled my face against her fur. "You push the limit, little one. Remember, you have only four lives left."

She gave a meow of thanks, jumped to the ground, and bounded off toward a new adventure. There were times I envied Ella's freedom. No one told her what to do.

With a sigh, I picked up my skirts and resumed my search for my friend, Síofra. I knew where to find her. All I had to do was locate a circle of mushrooms that we called fairy rings. The best ones were found near the tower ruins on the hill overlooking our home. Síofra appointed herself the official guardian of the rings and placed palm-size stones around their perimeters. The stones helped identify the rings so humans wouldn't accidently stumble into one. According to Síofra, the Sidhe didn't like humans entering their world unannounced.

Legend predicted that time slowed for anyone who

entered the circle, and if they stayed too long, they risked disappearing into the Fairy Realm forever. There were days I thought that wouldn't be a bad thing. Being a Logan meant heavy responsibilities.

I turned off the path and headed toward a copse of oak trees. Just as I'd suspected, Síofra was near a fairy ring. Although the day was as gray as a newly forged sword, Síofra looked like she was bathed in rainbows. Her tunic-style dress was her design and made from panels of dyed wool. Shades of green apples, lavender fields, and the hues of blush-pink roses collided together in perfect harmony. Matching ribbons cascaded through her white-gold hair like glistening streams.

She never questioned me about how I could read the currents and the wind, or why I never got lost, and I never questioned her about how she knew so much about the fairies. She was our castle's expert when it came to the Sidhe, probably because it was whispered she was a Changeling.

I never liked the word.

Changelings were said to be deformed fairy children who were exchanged for a human baby. Some believed they brought bad luck. Mother called it superstitious nonsense. She said she took one look at Síofra's heart-shaped face and knew we couldn't abandon her like her own mother had.

Our cook, Mary Mac Duff, had found Síofra on our doorstep when she was only a few weeks old. She had been wrapped in a multi-colored blanket with her name embroidered in gold. The villagers believed she had been abandoned because of her withered right arm and hand. I never understood their reasoning.

We understood each other perfectly, finished each other's sentences, and shared our most secret dreams. Síofra wanted to be queen of the Sidhe, and, no surprise, I wanted to be a blood-thirsty pirate.

She moved aside enough for me to notice that she wasn't alone. She was talking to John Dee, a student from the school located on a large meadow outside the castle walls.

The school was named after the Celtic god, Oghma, who invented the early forms of writing in Ireland. Its formal name was Oghma Grain Aineach University of Bardic Champions. Naturally the students shortened it to Oghy U.

A wide variety of classes were offered. For those interested in becoming politicians or lawyers there were advanced classes on Brehon Law, Latin, Greek, writing, and mathematics. History and philosophy were taught, as well as the seven steps necessary for aspiring poets and bards.

The King of England, Henry VIII, wanted to close our school and others like it across Ireland. It didn't seem to matter to him that the Irish had kept the written word alive during the Dark Ages, when Europe had preached knowledge was dangerous and heretical. During that time, people from all over the world visited Ireland in order to attend the universities.

Mother said the King, after executing his fifth wife, and although in poor health, intended to marry again. I didn't know why this was good news until she explained that if the King were busy sorting out his personal life, he'd leave Ireland and our schools alone.

In one of the few times my parents had agreed on anything, they had announced that I was forbidden to attend Oghy U. And yes, not going to school with children my own age was as lonely as it sounded.

I stomped down the old wound and focused on my friend.

While Síofra reminded me of springtime, John Dee looked like winter had come early. He blended into the shadows and looked more like a shriveled old man than a lad of fifteen. He wore ankle-length, priest-like robes, had shaved his head, and was as thin and brittle as a dried birch twig. We didn't know his whole story, only that his father was a tailor to Henry the VIII and that he had been sent here against his will. Maybe that was why he said he preferred books to people.

Last year John Dee had lent me a book on the topic of how to foretell your future by charting the stars. Headmaster Mac Elatha reported the incident to my parents and they forbade both Síofra and I from further contact with John Dee. After that, the three of us were inseparable.

But for some reason John Dee avoided the topic of star charts, and I dropped the subject. If he knew my future, he kept it to himself.

John Dee clutched a leather-bound book in his arms and seemed agitated. "I won't give it back," he said to Síofra, his voice rising in panic.

"You must," Síofra insisted. "You stole it from Headmaster Mac Elatha."

"But that's just it," John Dee said. "*Lebor Gabála Érenn,* the *Book of Invasions* is not…" He must have heard me approach, because he stopped talking. His gaze shifted behind me. His eyes widened as though he'd seen a ghost. "I have to leave. You must meet me later tonight."

He took off down the hill in the direction of the school. His legs tangled in his robes as he ran, but he never lost his balance. Until today, I hadn't known he could move that fast. He was a little bookworm creature that did everything as slow as the seasons.

I was about to ask what she and John Dee had been discussing when I heard a familiar voice.

"After him!" Cooley, the village bully shouted. His brothers, Dun and Duib, raced down the hill after John Dee.

Cooley shoved his red cap farther down his forehead, shading his eyes while the other two raced after John Dee. He turned on Síofra like the barrel of a cannon. "What did the little insect tell you?"

Síofra held her withered arm close against her waist. Her lower lip trembled as she raised her chin. She was the kindest person I knew. Before today, the Herding Boys had avoided her. For some reason that had changed.

I stepped between them. "Leave my friend alone or I'll...I'll..." I couldn't think of any threat he'd believe, and my voice shook so badly I doubted I'd make sense even if I could come up with something clever.

They were from a village on the west coast of Ireland. Their chief form of entertainment was to corner and bully students and small animals. Ella hissed whenever she saw the trio. We'd nicknamed them the Herding Boys for the obvious reason that they liked to herd things—animals, people, insects. They were always together, wore mud-colored tunics, and despite their varying heights, looked exactly alike. They had bushy hair that hung over their faces and eyebrows that grew together in one continuous line.

Nobody liked them, but when we complained to the professors, Headmaster Mac Elatha said we had to try and get along as we were all Children of Danu. That meant the subject was closed.

I'd never confronted Cooley or his brothers before, and that made me feel like a coward. I'd seen what happened to students who had. Some ended up in trees. Others were forced to eat earthworms. Nothing life-threatening, but scary all the same. One day, we thought they'd cross the line and someone would get hurt. Even Mother was afraid of them.

"This does not concern you," he said evenly, turning on me. "You should leave while I'm feeling generous." And then he laughed, scaring a flock of starlings out of the trees. He leaned in until he towered over me like the shadow of a menacing giant. "My business is with Síofra and John Dee."

I felt her hand on my shoulder and her whispered plea for me to leave. Did I mention they liked pulling wings off butterflies?

"I'm not leaving you alone with Cooley," I said to my friend, but I knew my voice didn't sound as brave as my words.

Dun and Duib returned out of breath. "John Dee disappeared," they both said at the same time.

Cooley hesitated, tearing his gaze from mine long enough to cuff the brother closest to him. Duib flew through the air as though he were no heavier than bird feathers and slammed against the trunk of a tree.

Síofra and I stepped back.

"This is the last time I'll ask nicely," he said. "What did John Dee tell you? Was it about the Book? If you don't…"

The bells in the castle tower tolled. They echoed over the valley like the voice of doom. The sound drowned out the waves crashing against the cliffs below and the pounding of my heart. A new fear took hold.

Our bells tolled for only one reason.

We were under attack.

Cooley and his brothers took off in the opposite direction of the castle, while Síofra and I stood paralyzed with fear. My father had said our home was safe.

"You must leave at once," Síofra said in the gentle way she had. "I will find John Dee."

I shivered. I had the strangest impression that John Dee and the attack were connected.

Chapter Two

I raced across the cliffs and entered the castle. Normally, the guards would have nodded a quick greeting or called out to me by name. Not this evening. Their grim expressions did nothing to calm my growing panic as I skidded to a stop in the Great Hall.

Our castle was fortified, and our root cellars stocked for a long siege. Even so, attacks from the sea were one of our greatest fears. A well-aimed cannon blast could crumble the walls to dust and leave us vulnerable. But fear of an attack vanished as another one took its place.

It was too quiet.

Fires were built to chase away the autumn chill in twin hearths large enough to roast a full-grown cow with room to spare. They faced each other from either side of the room like angry warriors trying to out-blaze the other.

The large trestle table where we took our meals stood barren. Somber-faced warlords gathered at the far end of the hall. My first thought was war, but the chieftains weren't raising their fists or clanging their weapons against their shields as I'd seen in the past.

They were afraid. I could taste it on the air. It was charged with energy like the calm before a storm.

I stretched on tiptoes to my full height but couldn't see above the men huddled in a tight circle. One thing was certain: they were talking to someone and becoming more agitated by the minute.

My mother stood off to the side, as regal and calm as a queen expecting nobles from the Spanish court. Her gown was made from yards of heavy worsted wool with thick tubular folds. It was the color of saffron and brought out the gold highlights in her red, waist-length hair. Worry lines creased her smooth complexion. Her gaze told me everything I needed to know. Something had happened to Father.

She turned away and disappeared into the tight circle of men.

I walked across the stone floors. Each step echoed, drawing me close. The hum of conversation turned to grumbling and angry words. When I reached the gathering, I thought the warlords would block my path. I needn't have worried.

Their shouts scorched the air.

"Brain-soaked boy," a bear of a chieftain yelled.

"Fool," said a man with only one arm.

"Impossible tale," said a third and received a mumbled agreement from the group.

"Goblins are stories to scare little children," said a fourth man with an eye patch. "They do not exist."

All the other comments had drawn fevered debate. The last one was met with stone silence. Ireland, despite its outward protests, believed in its legends.

I drew in a breath.

A few of the warlords made the sign of the cross, and the rest mouthed prayers.

I shouldered my way past the chieftains of the Burke and O'Tool clans. These men were Father's closest friends. They gave my mother a troubled glance and then followed their comrades retreating from the Great Hall.

As I reached her side, I noticed she was talking to a young man and handed him something that he palmed and slipped into his shirt. He was seated on a chair and looked around my age. She gave him a mug of steaming buttermilk and placed her hand on his shoulder. The gesture troubled me more than the chieftain's words.

Mother had a generous nature, but over the last few years she'd grown distant and spent more and more time alone. When I was little, she'd cared for strays of every kind, both men and beast. I wondered what had rekindled her kindness. As she stepped to the side, she seemed to notice me for the first time.

"Granuaile." My mother's voice was strained and her face pale. "You should not be here."

Perhaps it was her use of the formal version of my name, or something I couldn't define, but I couldn't leave. I glanced toward the young man who had been the center of attention. He was soaked to the bone as though he'd just emerged from the water. Seaweed clung to his clothes and shoulder-length hair that was as black as the cliffs of Moher. But that wasn't the oddest part: Ella lay curled asleep on his bare feet as though they were old friends. Ella didn't usually like strangers.

I lowered my voice, trying not to dwell on my growing apprehension. Or why Mother continued to shut me out. "Who is he?" I asked with newfound courage.

She hesitated and stared at him for a long time. For some reason, I thought I noticed a silent communication pass between them. "His name is Mac Tíre," she said at last. "He served on Dark Oak's ship, and barely escaped with his life. He was thrown overboard in the explosion."

"Explosion?" My stomach tightened. Dark Oak was the name everyone called Father. Mother, on the other hand, only called him Michale. She seemed more distant than usual, as though she were drifting away, as though in her heart she'd already said her good-byes to him.

I felt I had lost both parents. Father lived a dangerous life. He never liked us to call him a pirate, but that's what he was. He and his crew were gone for months at a time. He attacked merchant ships returning from the Americas and as a result made enemies of France, Spain, and even England. On occasion, he even caused mischief—his word not mine—with some of the other Irish warlords. Mischief was his word for "attack."

I swallowed down the lump of panic. "What happened to Father?"

Mother straightened her shoulders as though trying to regain her balance. "It's best you hear it from Mac Tíre."

His eyes were ice blue and he was so tall I had to tilt my head to meet his gaze. He set his mug beside our cat and said, "The last thing I remember was that I was thrown into the water, and when I surfaced, *The Red Branch,* your father, and his crew had vanished."

Chapter Three

With Ella on my heels, I ran blindly through the castle's corridors, leaving Mac Tíre and Mother far behind. The smell of fresh baked bread was weaving toward me even before I realized I was headed toward the cookroom. Mary was kneading bread, while more baked in the brick oven. A fine mist of flour coated the air as she hummed a tune.

Ella padded over to her bed by the fire as though nothing out of the ordinary had happened. Mary's husband, Jamie, had brought Ella back with him from one of his voyages to the Isle of Man. The breed had pointed ears and the Irish believed they were created by fairies. Jamie had named the kitten Ella, which means little elf, or elfin.

In preparation for the celebration of Samhain, Mary had hollowed out pumpkins, white turnips, and yellow squash, and then carved faces. She'd perched them in rows along the edge of a bench, like parishioners kneeling behind a pew. There was a lighted candle inside the one on the end. His expression was carved to look frightened. He looked like he'd seen the Death Coach.

I shivered and turned to leave.

"Slow down, lass," Mary said in her thick Scottish brogue, the sound round and full of laughter. "Stay for a while."

Her tone made me feel a little better. She and her husband, Jamie, had arrived from Scotland before I was born. Her husband was hired on as a crewmember on one of Father's ships. Mary supplied our castle with pies and breads. When Jamie died at sea, ten years ago, Mother offered Mary a job as our cook. She'd woven into our lives like the threads on a tapestry and become like a grandmother to me. In many ways I felt closer to her than my own mother.

"A fine lot this year, if I do say so myself," Mary continued, motioning over to the pumpkins as though unaware of my silence. "Their fierce expressions will make sure the ghosts and beasties stay away. Do ye have a favorite?"

"I could have used one in my room last night," I mumbled under my breath. When Mary held out her arms, I ran straight into her comforting embrace.

She patted me on the head as I snuggled into her warmth. "What is wrong, lassie? Ye are shaking like a leaf in a windstorm."

I pulled away, unable to form the words as if saying them aloud would make them true.

She gently disentangled me from her arms and led me over to the table. Wedges of baked piecrust were arranged on a pewter plate. Flaky and sprinkled with cinnamon, they were my favorite treats. I shouldn't have been surprised. She always seemed to know when I'd pay her a visit.

She poured buttermilk into a mug made from a hollowed-out elk's horn and pressed it into my hands. "Is this about yer father's ship?"

My stomach clenched into knots again as I wrapped my fingers around the horn of buttermilk. I wanted to ask her about the Banshee we called Cally, but I was concerned it would bring back bad memories.

She wiped her hands on her apron and shook her head in disgust. "Yer father's chieftains exploded into my cookroom as though they were running from the Headless Horseman himself. Almost trampled me under their great muddy boots, they did." Her expression gentled. "What do ye think of the lad's story?"

I wasn't sure. I took a bite of the crust to delay answering. It melted in my mouth and brought back fond childhood memories. The cookroom and Mary were a protected corner of the castle where I could be myself. Where I could feel safe. I set the crust down.

"Mac Tíre claimed Father was captured."

"Captured is not killed," said the practical Mary. "And who's saying he's dead? I heard the lad said the ship disappeared like my pies on feast day."

I nodded, but I couldn't shake the expression in my mother's eyes. "Yes, captured is not killed," I repeated in an attempt to make the words bring me strength. It didn't work.

"And yet," Mary said, "yer father's warlords, instead of mounting a rescue, are headed to the local pub or hiding in their cottages. For all their bluster, they believe Mac Tíre's story."

My throat tightened as I glanced down at the uneaten crust. "Mac Tíre said..." I hesitated, taking a deep breath. "Mac Tíre said something about spells."

"And what did your mother have to say?"

I shook my head.

Mary brushed an imaginary smudge off her apron. "Yer dear mother has a lot on her mind these days, poor lass. Well, 'tis up to me, then." She reached into a cupboard and drew out a leather pouch.

"I've kept this for you…just in case. Inside are protections as well as healing herbs. Each individual pouch is labeled with the names of the herb and its purpose." She cinched the leather pouch to my belt. "Make sure ye keep it with ye always." She smiled, selecting a few piecrusts off my plate and wrapping them in a cloth. "I'll even add yer treats."

I nodded, not saying a word. I'd learned from experience that refusing to accept medicines, herbs or even food from Mary was a waste of time. Her reasoning always prevailed.

Even so, Mary was acting strangely, and I was worried. She was like this whenever someone mentioned spells, magic…or the Sidhe. I stood on my tip toes and kissed her on the cheek. "We Irish are as silly as cats around Samhain. You're right. Captured is not killed. I'm sorry I worried you."

Mary stared at the amber flames. "A spell is about. The lad only confirmed what I already felt. His presence on the ship might be the reason the crew was captured and not killed. My Jamie always said having someone like Mac Tíre onboard with ancient Irish bloodlines was a precaution. A Selkie is best of course, as they have the strongest connection to the sea. Now, I'm not saying the lad's a Selkie. In fact, I'm pretty sure if he was he would not have returned to shore, still…"

I sat up straighter. Did Mary think Mac Tíre was a member of the Sidhe? Impossible. More likely it was Mary's resurfacing of her grief that had taken her down this road. This always happened whenever there was news of a ship wreck. I knew Mary's faraway expression meant that she was thinking about Jamie.

To try and distract her, I said, "You've never told me about Selkies."

As I'd hoped, Mary brushed a tear from her cheek as her expression lightened. "I can't believe I haven't mentioned Selkies before. Why, they're the most magical creatures of them all. They're seals, of course and can change into human form at will. Beautiful creatures. Many's the man who longs to catch one and make her his wife. But he must hide her pelt if he wants her to stay with him. The sea is their first love and is more powerful than mortal love. There wasn't anyone with even a drop of Sidhe blood onboard Jamie's last voyage and I knew he was worried. Told me so on the night before he left. My Jamie wasn't the only sailor to die on that voyage. Yer father returned with only half his crew." She shook her head. "They should have had someone like Mac Tíre onboard."

Talking about Irish myths and legends had not proven to be the distraction I'd hoped. *The Red Branch* and its crew had disappeared, and no one seemed concerned or interested in launching a rescue. Instead, all everyone talked about were spells and moldy old legends.

I jabbed the remaining piecrust on my plate into crumbs, trying to keep my temper in check. "My father and his crew are still missing, but because of him, and the tale he told, everyone is afraid."

"As well they should. I'm not sure of Mac Tíre's exact connection to the Sidhe," Mary said, wagging her finger at me, "but Ella was running in circles the moment he arrived. I have never seen her so excited. And make no mistake, your mother is not telling the whole story."

I shoved my plate aside. "Why would she do such a thing?"

Mary shook her head. "All I know is that there are all manner of secrets connected to this castle and your family, and sooner or later, they will all come tumbling out."

****

Ella meowed so loud, the sound woke the cat with a start. Ella stretched out her paws and yawned. Her actions were so humanlike, it made both Mary and I laugh, easing the tension. We used to joke that Ella didn't act like any of our other cats. It was not just her fascination with water. She stared at you as though she knew something no one else knew.

The cat yawned again and glanced over at me. Her gold eyes glowed in the candle light. Her gaze narrowed slightly as though she were about to speak.

It was the oddest sensation. In that moment I thought her eyes changed color, from gold to a more human shade of green. But when I blinked, the illusion vanished. Then Ella did a more cat-like thing. She licked her paw and ignored us as though we were no more important than dust bunnies.

The entertainment over, Mary started cleaning the cutting table. The pumpkin with the frightened expression glowed brighter. I tilted my head in its direction. "Why did you light only one of the gourds?"

"I haven't lit any of them, lassie. I was waiting until All Hollows' Eve. I won't waste a good candle." She'd turned her back to me as she scooped pumpkin seeds onto a sheet for roasting. There was a smile in her voice as she spoke. "Ye are seeing things. Have ye been rubbing your eyelids with marigold water?"

She referred to an old superstition. Marigold blossoms helped a person see into the fairy realm. "That method doesn't work," I muttered. "I tried."

A sudden gust of wind lashed against the windows and the shutters banged the outside walls. In the next moment, the candle in the pumpkin snuffed out. The wind howled, exactly as it had last night. It pierced the night like the wails at a funeral.

I slid off the stool and bumped into Ella. Instead of protesting, she wove through my legs, indicating she wanted me to pick her up. Grateful, I obliged, gathering her in my arms. She nuzzled against me as the wails turned to moans.

It wasn't that Ireland didn't have storms. We had more than our share, especially in October. But it didn't always mean the onset of a storm. It could mean something far worse.

"It's only the wind," I whispered against Ella's fur. "No one's going to die."

Mary stood near the hearth and was so still I thought she was anchored to the floor. Her eyes were almost as wide as the ones she'd carved into the pumpkins. If there was one person who recognized the difference between the wail of the wind and a Banshee, it was Mary. She'd heard the Banshee's call the night her husband had died.

She glanced toward me with an odd expression that made me uneasy. I'd rarely seen Mary so worried. Her silence confirmed my fears. To the outside world, she appeared to have taken her husband's death in stride, saying she knew the life he led was dangerous. They'd been married a long time and had been childhood sweethearts. She had said her only regret was losing their babe the night he was born. Mary maintained their child was waiting for them in one of the four cities of Tir na nÓg, known as the Land of the Forever Young.

"The Banshee predicts death," Mary said, her voice catching on the last word.

The wail rattled the shutters again and seemed closer. I handed the cat to Mary and rushed over to the window. The night was draped in black like a shroud pulled over a coffin. The wind howled, blowing the clouds so only a sliver of the moon shone through. The outline of a woman floated in the branches like white foam on a jet-black sea. My heart racing, I slammed and bolted the shutters closed.

"I remember where I was when the Banshee first appeared," Mary said, her voice as whisper-thin as Irish mist. "I was in my cottage. The one Jamie built for us. 'Twas a fine place. A snug thatched roof with thick walls. The fire burned a cheerful amber-red, like tonight. I heard the Banshee's wail and even before I went to the window, I knew. There she was, hovering in the air, a wisp of white smoke and sad eyes. To this day I can't tell ye what she said, except I knew Jamie had died suddenly and that he hadn't suffered."

She tucked Ella in the crook of her arm and reached for an iron poker with her free hand. She shoved a square of the peat we used as fuel for the fire back into place. "When your father returned, he told me that when the storm struck, the main mast broke off and hit Jamie in the head. My lovely man died instantly. But of course, I knew that already."

I thought of Father and Mac Tíre's story. I didn't want to believe spells were possible. Reality seemed easier to fight. Father knew how to defend an attack by a Spanish warship or survive a storm. How could he fight magic?

"Maybe it's just a warning," I said with hope. "I've heard she does that sometimes."

Mary let out a sigh. "How I wish that were true, but in my experience a Banshee's wail means one thing. Someone will die."

Chapter Four

The Irish don't say it was raining. We say it was a soft day. Most places, when it rains, it feels like a giant tossed out a bucket of wash water. In Ireland, rain is as soft as if it were made from mist and fairy kisses. Despite the romanticized version, the morning was gray and getting grayer as the day grew older. What was worse, I'd received a summons from my mother.

Ella and I waited in the doorway for her to invite us inside. When she nodded, I entered slowly as Ella trotted over to the windowsill. My mother's chamber was a sea of green velvet and blue silk. Despite my father's warning that large windows made her quarters vulnerable to attack, she went ahead with her plans. She'd insisted the walls that faced the ocean be replaced with floor to ceiling leaded glass. As a result, even in the dark of winter, her rooms were flooded with light. Usually they cheered me up, but after a nod from my mother to enter, the rooms looked darker than normal.

She was near the windows, mumbling in ancient Irish. The gold charms on her bracelet moved as she worked, and it sounded like the music of wind chimes on a summer's eve. She placed sliced apples and hazelnuts on the sills and lavender on the window benches.

According to legend, the *Marbh Bhee*, or Walking

Dead were released from the Otherworld during the days leading up to All Hollows' Eve. They roamed throughout the countryside looking for food to bring back with them to their underground realm. The offerings placed on a threshold prevented them from entering the homes of the living.

I'd watched her perform this ritual for as long as I could remember and never had given it much thought. It was one of the countless superstitious that was a part of my life. A sick person's bed should be placed north and south, not crossways. Never cut your hair on a Friday. Never begin a journey on a Saturday or if the moon is full. Or was it a Wednesday with a crescent moon? I could never keep them all straight.

But the food my mother left always disappeared. I'd thought one of our wolfhounds or a homeless wanderer, too proud to beg for food, was to blame. But what if the superstitions worked the way she said?

I rubbed my arms, attempting to dismiss the Banshee and the sudden chill prickling my skin. Trying not to think of something only made you think of it more.

"You wanted to speak with me?" I said.

Mother stepped back from the window. Her hands laced together like interlocking Celtic knots. "Your birthday is only a week away. There are things we need to discuss."

Mother glanced toward Ella on the window sill and heaved a sigh. "Shouldn't you be catching mice?"

Mother spoke to Ella as though she were a real person, but only when Father wasn't around.

Unfazed, Ella sat back on her haunches and cleaned her paws.

Mother shook her head and turned her attention on me. "As you are aware, the O'Brien chieftain and his son have agreed to your father's marriage terms and will arrive on Samhain." She made the statement as though she were announcing the menu for tonight's evening meal. I stiffened as she continued. "The union will strengthen your father's position and add lands to his treasury."

I clenched my fists together. "Síofra says the Sidhe fairies can marry anyone they choose."

Mother flicked a glance toward Ella, who'd paused in her cleaning ritual. "Your best friend shouldn't tell you such tales."

There was a time when Mother was as enthralled as I was about Síofra's tales.

"It is time you grew up," she continued. "You are the daughter of an Irish chieftain and with privilege comes responsibility."

And there it was, my mother's last words on the subject. Not that I'd mind getting married—someday— to a great fighter, like the legendary Irish warrior Cuchulainn, or a solder-prince from a faraway land. But before marriage I wanted to captain my own ship and sail to exotic lands. If I was destined to have the same life as Mother's, I wanted to have adventures first.

I took in a deep breath, feeling guilty. Father was captured, Cally had appeared to me twice, and all I was thinking about was me. I'd always known this day would come, but I wouldn't be getting married right away. Betrothals and arranged marriages could last five or ten years before the actual ceremony. If you were lucky, the guy changed his mind. Not very often if your father were as rich as mine, but there was always that hope.

I raised my chin, determined not to complain. I was turning fifteen in a week. Time to grow up, but even so, my practical self argued that getting married wasn't as important as finding Father. Knowing full well a big part of me was using this as a delay maneuver, I blurted, "When will they send out a rescue party?"

She shook her head absently. The charms on her bracelet chimed together as she walked over to the trunk at the foot of her bed. Father gave her a new charm each time he returned from a voyage or for a special occasion. Each one was unique. When I was a child we used to sit for long hours and she would tell me the story behind each one. I missed those days.

She fingered one shaped like a small harp. "The chieftains feel it is too dangerous to send out a ship in this weather." As she knelt, her skirts billowed around her over the sprigs of lavender that covered the floor. She opened the lid of the bench seat and motioned for me to join her.

Resting on a pillow of silk was the wooden box where she kept her keepsakes. A wreath made from wildflowers that she'd worn on her wedding day. A lace collar from her dress. A jeweled knife inside a leather sheath. A silver locket. A gold ring.

She hesitated for a moment and then reached for the ring. I admit it—I was hoping for the knife. Jewelry wasn't really my thing. Jewelry clanked and jingled and got in the way at sword practice. Even so, I moved forward to get a closer look. It was solid gold, with the image of marigolds etched into the band and inlaid with yellow and green enamel. Celtic swirls and symbols covered the inside of the circle. It was breathtaking, and this from someone who didn't like jewelry.

"It has been in my family longer than memory," my mother explained, holding out the ring. "It is given the week before an eldest daughter reaches her fifteenth birthday. But beware. This ring has a cost. You may keep it for as long as you wish, but the moment you slip the ring on your finger, the veil between realms will lift and you will see the world as it is, not as you wish it to be." She hesitated as she fingered the ring in the palm of her hand. "This is a big step. Perhaps you're not ready."

A chilled breeze swept in from the open window as though in warning. I ignored it and snatched the ring from her hand before she could change her mind. I had no idea what she was talking about, but she'd offered me something that had belonged to her family. She'd never talked about her family, no matter how many times I asked her about her life before she met Father. This was the first connection I would have with her family, and I wasn't about to let it go.

"Thank you," I said, praying that was the right thing to say.

Silently, she drew me into an embrace. Her tears dampened my cheeks as she kissed me and then she moved toward her favorite window seat overlooking the pounding surf.

I stared down at the ring as my vision blurred. Searching for a way to prolong my visit, I said, "I heard the Banshee's wail."

Her shoulders stiffened. "You are late for breakfast and your lesson with your new tutor. Please remember that no matter what happens, I will always love you."

****

Food was the last thing on my mind. A close second was meeting with a new tutor. I dragged my feet along the dimly lit corridors as I rolled the ring in the palm of my hand. The enamel in the flowers was darker than a few minutes ago, more red than yellow.

When Mother said she loved me, it had felt like she was saying goodbye, and the ring was her parting gift. I could see it in her expression. I had to be mistaken. After all, it was only jewelry.

I shoved it on before I could change my mind, turned the corner, and plowed into John Dee. I was surprised to see him. My parents had made it clear that he wasn't welcome in our castle.

He seemed as startled as I was and dropped the book he was carrying. It landed on the floor and opened to a page with illuminated lettering and Celtic designs. The book looked like the one he'd had yesterday when he was running from the Herding Boys.

On the page, a woman dressed for battle rode a charging horse across a field. Perched on her shoulder was a raven, as black as the deepest cave. Her face was turned in my direction and seemed to meet my gaze. I shuddered and looked away. It had to be an illusion.

"Her name is Epona, the Horse Goddess," John Dee said. Sweat beaded on his forehead as he snatched the book off the floor. He clutched it so tightly, his knuckles shone as white as a linen sheet. "I am not doing this for myself."

I didn't have the chance to ask him what he'd meant. Just then a shadow caught my attention. When I turned back, John Dee was gone.

Chapter Five

When I reached the castle's only classroom, a guard was posted outside. Security had increased since Mac Tíre's arrival.

Paddy smiled down at me. "Good morning, lass."

I nodded a half-hearted response. I dreaded meeting another new tutor. Five this year, and I had two months to go. I tended to be more interested in the stories of warriors than in learning ancient languages like Latin or Greek. My excuse was that we weren't at war with Rome or Greece. Those nations had long since lost their power, so the few people who spoke their languages were either priests, nobles, or those interested in reading ancient texts. I was none of the three. I didn't see the point and therefore the tutors became frustrated and quit.

"Is he in good spirits?" I asked Paddy, nodding to the closed door. I'd known Paddy all my life. He'd been with our family since before I had been born and had fought alongside my father in countess battles. Good-natured and as round as he was tall, Paddy had the sort of chuckle that made you want to laugh along, whether you understood the jest or not.

Paddy lifted a bushy eyebrow. All signs of his good-natured disposition vanished. "Not much of a talker. Mary heard him enter only after Ella created a fuss. He insisted I show him to the classroom." He patted the sword strapped to his belt. "Leave the door ajar. I'm here if you need me."

Paddy opened the door for me. Maybe he sensed he'd have to, since he knew I'd skip class if given the chance.

****

My mother had decorated the classroom herself. Tapestries, with images of people reading, writing, or reciting poetry hung on the walls to keep out the dampness as well as to inspire learning. A fire blazed in the snug hearth and torches were lit to chase away the morning gloom. There was a bookshelf on the wall by the window as well as a table and bench. I was convinced the furniture was made uncomfortable on purpose so I wouldn't fall asleep. Everything appeared as it always had, but I couldn't shake the feeling that something was missing.

The tutor was tucked in the shadows by the window, his back toward me. Tall and reed-thin, he gazed toward the sea. His head was covered in the hood of an ankle length robe. It struck me that he looked like a taller version of John Dee. Aside from the resemblance to my friend, he fit the description of every other tutor or professor I'd ever met. Which meant he probably wore spectacles, never smiled, and liked giving homework.

I cleared my throat to catch his attention. He mumbled in a voice that rolled and sloshed like clams in a bucket of seawater. Something about my being late. Something about this being beneath his station. The usual.

"You can call me Mr. Aillén. I was told you have an interest in the first kings and queens of Ireland," he said without turning. "Name Ireland's first ruler."

I puffed up my chest. I knew this question. "The first king of Ireland was Brian Boru."

He made a noise that sounded a lot like a growl. "Wrong. Boru was an imposter. Crom Dubh, known as The Dragon, was the first to unite Ireland. Let us see if you can do better at solving puzzles."

He turned from the window then glided into the center of the room. Glide was the only way to describe how he moved. Then I caught his smell. Rotting seaweed and dead fish. His features were shrouded in the depths of his hood.

"To test your knowledge of Irish history, you must guess my…disguise. And, so help me child, if you say I'm a vain Tuatha de Danaan, I'll turn you into a cat without claws."

A chill chased down my spine. The threat sounded real, as though he had that kind of power. I reminded myself that this was a game. I stood taller. "You're talking about casting spells. Are you a Druid?" I asked, although something about the slope of his shoulders and the shape of his head didn't fit.

"A Druid? You insult me. Druids once were leaders, wielding enormous power. Now they are little more than actors, and magicians doing sleight of hand and card tricks. I admit a few are above average. For example, Mug Ruith and his flying machines. But he's switched allegiances so often no one trusts him anymore, which is why he and his sorceress daughter aren't speaking."

He wasn't Tuatha or a Druid. I searched my memory of Ireland's history. "Did you represent one of Ireland's invaders?"

"A good question. My kind were seafarers from Northern Africa. We represent chaos and wild nature versus the Tuatha de Danaan who represent human civilizations. One of our kings invented writing. Did we get credit? Of course not." His voice sounded hurt, which seemed odd because he was just playing a part.

"We and the Tuatha married," he continued, "and had children together until we were tricked by one of our own kind and driven under the sea."

He rambled on and on about ancient history and forgotten battles. Exactly the topics tutors love. I relaxed and focused on solving the riddle. "Firbolg," I offered. "They ruled Ireland before the arrival of the Tuatha and Femorians."

"The Firbolgs are cowards," he said as though he'd bitten into a mushy apple. He glanced toward the window as though he were keeping track of the time by measuring how high the sun had risen over the water. "The Tuatha allowed Firbolgs to settle in the Connacht region. Troublesome bunch. The whole lot." For a moment I couldn't tell whether he meant the Firbolgs or the Tuatha until I remembered my history.

"The Firbolgs were banished to the Aran Islands."

"Not all."

I felt the sudden urge to defend these people. "Weren't a few of them advisors to the Tuatha?"

"The Tuathan obsession with beauty led to their downfall." His angry tone heated the air with venom.

I shifted weight. Most tutors were passionate about their topics. He took it to a new level. It was personal. "The Tuatha aren't so bad," I insisted. "The Red Branch champions: Cuchulainn, Queen Maeve…"

He dismissed the heroes and heroines of Ireland

with a flick of his wrist. "I'm Femorian, you half-wit."

He was across the room, but it felt as if his hands were around my throat, squeezing.

"Femorians were tyrants," I said, finally tired of his misrepresentation of my heroes and heroines. "Their last ruler tricked his grandfather, Balor of the Evil Eye, into joining him in a war against the Tuatha. The Tuathan champion, Lugh of the Long Arm, defeated Balor and the war ended in a Tuathan victory."

He moved in closer. "You forgot the part where the Femorians were banished to the sea."

The tutor flipped off his hood. It took a moment to register. He had only one eye. It bulged in the center of his face like a full moon and his teeth were filed into sharp points.

I backed toward the door. My heart hammered in my ears. Was he wearing a mask? Mary said throughout Europe, the courts of the kings and queens held elaborate balls where everyone dressed in costumes. If this was a disguise, it was the best one I'd ever seen.

But I knew it wasn't.

The walls closed in. "You only…"

"Have one eye," he finished. He chuckled like I imagined a crow might laugh if it knew how. He wasn't pretending to be a Femorian. He was a Femorian.

I screamed.

A loud meow pierced the air. It came from the direction of the hallway outside the classroom. In the space between the floor and bottom of the door, Ella continued to meow as she paced back and forth.

Paddy shouted my name and pounded against the door. "Open the door. That man is not your tutor." The thin oak panels vibrated under his fists but didn't give way. Paddy yelled for me to step aside and warned he meant to break in, while Ella hissed and clawed at the door.

Ella's hisses turned to growls.

The tutor spoke through gritted teeth. "No one told me you had a cat from the Isle of Man." He raised his arm and the noise outside the chamber walls ceased.

****

The classroom exploded in light.

The force knocked me to the floor. I held my head, trying to stay grounded as the room spun in a kaleidoscope of reds, oranges, and blacks. It was so quiet I could hear my ragged breathing.

"How is this possible?" the tutor thundered. "You should be asleep. My spells never fail."

My head pounded as loudly as the door had moments before. I pushed to my feet. How had his appearance escaped Paddy? Or Mother?

A fog-like mist rose around him as he drew his crescent-shaped sword from the folds of his robes. His blade glistened like wet steel newly forged. "I was told not to underestimate you. To make sure you were alone when I killed you. Who protects you?"

I backed against the door, reaching for the handle. It turned, but the latch wouldn't release. I banged on the thick oak paneling and yelled for Paddy's help. There was no sound. I couldn't hear the door bang. I couldn't hear my voice. It was as though the room was muffled in thick layers of sheep wool. The only sound was the swishing of my tutor's sword as his blade cut through the air.

"Your guard cannot hear you," he said. "No one can. I also cast a special spell for that cat of yours."

I spun around to face him. I pressed against the door as though I could draw strength from the ancient oak wood.

"Are you one of my father's enemies, here to seek revenge? If you kill me, nothing will save you. He will hunt you down." The words were easy to say because they were true. My father might not be around much, but nothing was more important to him than family.

"Dark Oak and those like him will have more to worry about than seeking revenge for one life, even yours. The Goblins rise. War is coming. The survival of the human race hangs in the balance." He chuckled as though remembering a private jest. The shrill sound grated against my skin. "Your father is…contained."

"You know where he is?" My heart raced. Hope bubbled to the surface. I clung to the image of my father, safe and back home.

"You should be more concerned for yourself. That's why I'm here. Loose ends."

The threat hit me like cold water. I sucked in my breath, confused. "Loose ends?" I asked.

His gaze narrowed as though assessing his victim. My father's sword master drilled his students that too many warriors focused on an opponent's weapon instead of where they were looking. If the moment before your opponent attacked, he gazed toward your shoulder or midsection, that was his target.

I hoped the sword master was right.

So, when the Femorian glanced in the direction of my head as though he meant to cut it off, I was ready. As he raised his blade, I ducked, dropped to the ground, and rolled out of the way toward the windows.

I realized why I'd thought something in the

35

classroom was missing when I'd first entered. Usually, there were iron pokers near the fireplace and wood in the firebox. The area was stripped clean. Even the crossed swords that hung over the mantel were gone. My father had hung the weapons there as a reminder that warfare was part of the Logan heritage.

The tutor's sneer widened. "Yes, I removed anything you could use as weapon. I've lived this long as an assassin because I never underestimate my prey. Prepare to die."

I was on my own. No one would hear me scream.

****

I edged toward the largest window in the classroom.

Sunlight broke through the morning glum, pointing a ribbon of light at the feet of my tutor. Our castle was built on a cliff and its walls emptied into the base of jagged rocks and boiling sea. Waves crashed against the fortress as though reaching toward me.

If I jumped, I'd have to leap past the solid rock shelf. Unless I sprouted wings, I'd never make it. There was a slim chance the fall wouldn't break every bone in my body. I could walk away. Well, maybe not walk.

Mr. Aillén shielded his eye against the sun with his cupped hand. "You cannot run from me," he said, sensing my thoughts. "At the end, my victims are alike. They want to draw out the inevitability of their death. Accept your fate. I have more to lose than you, which makes me more motivated, more dangerous."

"You plan to kill me. I'm plenty motivated."

But something he'd said caught my attention. "What terrible thing will happen to you if you don't kill me?" I was stalling for time, exactly as he'd predicted.

The realization wasn't comforting.

His eye flicked for a brief second toward the window as though fearing he was watched. "If I fail, he'll send someone else to take my place."

"Who sent you?" I moved a few steps to my right, blocking the rays of the morning sun, testing a theory.

He seemed to relax and dropped his hand. "You ask too many questions."

"Annoying habit. Why do you want to kill me?"

"Epona's prophesy. They can't take any chances. Stand still and accept your fate. I promise it will be a quick death."

I didn't trust him. But this time I had another reason to stall for time. "You promise I won't feel anything?"

He smirked. "Only the bite of the sword, then blessed forever sleep."

The tutor charged.

I stepped out of the path of the sun.

The rays blinded him, but his momentum propelled him forward.

I stuck out my foot.

His eye flicked down and widened. Too late he tried to recover his balance. Tripping over my leg, he sailed through the open window.

He screamed a colorful litany of oaths that would have made a seaman blush. His sword flew out of his grasp. His arms flapped in the air like a robin being chased by a crow as his robes floated around him, tangling in his legs.

His flight was short. His body hit the rocks.

I flinched and squeezed my eyes shut.

Chapter Six

When I opened my eyes, Mr. Aillén had disappeared. The surf must have pulled him out to sea and dragged him back to the ocean floor. Waves spread over the rocks, washing away any sign. I couldn't tear my gaze away. My tutor claimed he was a Femorian and had only one eye. Was any of that even possible?

Maybe his threats to murder me clouded the whole experience. There was a plausible explanation. I had no problem believing Banshees existed, why not Femorians?

Well, whoever or whatever he was, I'd tripped him, and he'd fallen to his death.

True, he'd tried to kill me, but that didn't make me feel any better. I'd never hurt anyone or anything before today. I even picked up spiders and took them outside rather than squishing them under my foot.

Mr. Aillén had used the word *contained* in reference to my father. An odd choice. Not imprisoned, injured, or even dead, but contained. What did he mean?

Probably nothing. I was overthinking. Mary had said captured wasn't the same as killed, but if the stories about Femorians were true, my Father didn't have long to live. One thing was certain: I needed to stop overanalyzing a dead Femorian's word choice and ask my mother. Mary had claimed my mother wasn't telling the whole story.

The classroom door opened with little effort, making me think fear had caused me to imagine most of what had happened. That hope died in the next instant.

Paddy stood guard, resting against his staff. His breathing was shallow, and his eyes were unfocused as he stared past me, as though in a trance. Shivers raised the hair on my arms. I nudged him.

He crumpled to the ground like a rag doll. My fingers trembled as I checked for a pulse.

Alive.

Barely.

Normally, at this time of day the castle buzzed with activity. No sooner had one wing of the castle been cleaned than it was time to sweep another. There was a constant parade of villagers seeking advice on disputes and merchants bringing supplies. But the only sound was the wind whooshing through the corridors.

The cookroom was on the way to my mother's section of the castle, so I checked there first. Mary stood over the simmering stewpot. I called her name, but she didn't respond. Worried the flames might catch the hem of her skirts on fire, I pulled her to safety. It was like moving furniture. I kissed her on the cheek, choked back a sob, and bolted to my mother's wing.

I moved through the corridors in disbelief. The castle inhabitants, from servant to visiting chieftain, looked more like statues than living, breathing humans. They wore the same unfocused expression as Paddy and Mary.

When I arrived at my destination, the door to my mother's chamber had been left ajar. She sat at her favorite spot near the window, her back to me. The sight seemed so normal, I thought for a moment the spell hadn't reached this far.

"Mother. It's Grace."

When she didn't respond, I knew better. Her expression resembled the others with one exception. A single tear rested on her cheek. Had she known what was happening or was it something else?

My hands shook. I couldn't breathe. When my legs buckled, I reached out for the window ledge and missed.

****

I must have blacked out because when I awoke, Mac Tíre, the young man with the wild stories of spells and disappearing ships, pulled me to my feet.

"You're alive but you are not safe here. We have to leave."

I yanked away from him. Someone had just tried to kill me, my father was missing, and the castle was under a sleeping spell. There was no way I would trust a perfect stranger. "I'm not going anywhere with you."

The tapestry on the far wall rippled as though caught in the wind, exposing a hidden passageway. My mouth dropped open. I'd thought the entrances were boarded over.

Síofra emerged from behind the thick folds. Her expression looked relieved when she saw me. "Thank the Sidhe. Mac Tíre and I were looking for you."

Hoping it was a bad dream, I slid a glance toward my mother. She hadn't moved.

"We cannot help her," Síofra said.

I wanted to ask who could, but the words caught in my throat. What if the spell was permanent? I shuddered and wrapped my arms around myself.

"Did no one catch the part where I said we should leave?"

"Mac Tíre is correct," Síofra said. "You are not safe."

"How do you know him?" I said, feeling like a ship without a rudder. I swayed on my feet. Mac Tíre reached out to steady me, but I slapped his hand away and gave him my best *go away* expression. For the first time in my life I felt completely alone. Mac Tíre knew what was happening, and worse, so did Síofra. I was the only one left in the dark.

Mac Tíre tried to push me toward the passageway, but I side-stepped out of his reach. I wasn't leaving until I had answers. I crossed my arms over my chest. "What is going on?"

"We do not have much time," Síofra pleaded, glancing toward the door as though she expected armed soldiers to burst in at any moment. "Oghy U is in a panic. All the professors have disappeared, even Headmaster Mac Elatha."

Síofra picked at the threads on her sleeve. "We were coming to find you when we saw the Femorian assassin dive from your window and believed the worst. We thought we were too late."

I clenched my hands together, feeling shaky. "We can't be under attack," I pressed. "It's too quiet. No warning bells." I resisted the urge to glance over at my mother. Normally when we were under attack she made sure I was safe.

Síofra glanced over at Mac Tíre. They were keeping something from me. I didn't like secrets and it felt like I was drowning in them.

Síofra reached out and took my hand. "Everyone in

the castle is in an enchanted sleep. Mac Tíre and I were at the school when we realized what had happened."

"Not everyone is asleep," I reminded her. "I'm awake and so are you and…" I jerked my head in Mac Tíre's direction, "…him."

Síofra turned over my hand. "You're wearing your mother's ring."

Feeling guilty, I slipped my hand behind my back, wondering if I was supposed to wait until I turned fifteen. "Wait. How did you know she gave it to me?"

"Obviously, it helped protect her." Mac Tíre moved to the window. "Her mother must have suspected something like this might happen."

"But it only works if…" Síofra pressed her lips together and glanced uneasily over at Mac Tíre. "Why do you think they tried to kill her?"

Mac Tíre peered outside as though he'd heard something moving in the courtyard. For a moment I thought he intended to climb outside. His voice had a worried edge to it. "Three Femorians are headed our way. We can debate this at the school or stand and die. Your choice." He said it as though it didn't matter to him one way or the other.

Síofra peered outside. Her face turned pale. "The Herding Boys."

****

We chose to go to the school rather than stay and fight. Mac Tíre looked disappointed. It took me a moment to register that Síofra had identified the Herding Boys as Femorians.

Mac Tíre spread the tapestry's thick folds aside, exposing the entrance to the passageway. It yawned as black and dangerous as a predator's mouth. Taking one last look around my mother's chamber, I had a feeling I was leaving my childhood behind.

A labyrinth of secret corridors twisted behind the castle walls. When I was four or five, Mother had found me playing in one of them. In my defense I'd told her I wasn't alone or lost: I was with one of my imaginary friends. That had made it worse. The next day she had ordered all the entrances sealed.

Evidently, she'd missed one.

I lifted a torch from its holder. "I'm ready."

"No, you are not. Your mother should have prepared you. I will lead the way and Síofra will follow so you don't get lost. Do not fall behind." Mac Tíre snapped out orders as though he'd had a lot of practice, then disappeared into the jaw-like entrance.

"Is he always like this?" I said to Síofra. "Bossy?"

"He was assigned to protect you and was at Oghy U when you were attacked. He feels responsible."

I had a protector. I wasn't sure how I felt about that.

With Mac Tíre out front, and Síofra next in line, I ducked under the entrance and crossed the threshold. The passageway steps were narrow, uneven, and covered in slimy moss. Holding onto the walls for balance, I concentrated on not falling and walked into a tangle of spider webs. Wiping the clingy mess off my face, I was at least thankful for once that my mouth had been closed.

The passageway turned into a twisting labyrinth of corridors, just as I remembered. The odd thing was that I anticipated the turns Mac Tíre would make even before he made them. Already having played down here as a child must have been the reason, but that didn't explain how comfortable Mac Tíre was in the maze. Although I was the one with the torch, he was the one making decisions on which way to go as though he could see in the dark.

Around the next bend, I heard flowing water. An underground stream bubbled past us on its journey to the sea. Tucked in an alcove lay an abandoned boat as memories flooded back.

Mother never understood why I had spent so much time here when, in her words, I could be enjoying the sunshine. It was simple. Down here I was a captain, with a faithful crew: Ella and my imaginary friend. I couldn't remember his name or what he looked like, only the adventures we shared as we'd explored the underground waterways beneath the castle.

"I can see the exit," Mac Tíre announced over his shoulder as he disappeared around a corner.

"What's with that guy? Can he see in the dark?"

"We should hurry. I hear growling."

That caught my attention. "Growling?"

The corridor came to a dead end. Brick walls rose around us, closing off whatever lay beyond. Mac Tíre had disappeared.

"There," Síofra pointed toward pin-pricks of light. Pale moonlight, the color of cream, filtered through a thin curtain of ivy. The opening was narrow and not very high, as though made for children or small adults.

Muffled shouts erupted from the other side. I recognized Mac Tíre's voice, and then Cooley's.

How had the Herding Boys found us so quickly?

****

The Herding Boys had Mac Tíre surrounded. They were larger, as though they'd grown taller and put on

44

more weight since yesterday. Even more troubling was that they held clubs with spikes jutting out from the upper half. I'd never seen them with weapons of any kind. Their size was intimidating enough. That wasn't the only change. Just like my tutor Mr. Aillén, Cooley, Dun and Duib each had only one eye.

Why hadn't I seen this before? I twisted the ring on my finger that my mother had given me, remembering my mother's words. "The veil between worlds will lift and you will see the world as it is, not as you wish it to be."

Síofra eased in beside me to get a better look, and then sucked in her breath, sounding like a kettle giving off steam. "The Herding Boys said they would be on our side if war came. This is bad. This is very bad."

"We have sides?"

Cooley grumbled an order to Dun. Either to eat us or get us. Hard to tell.

Whichever one it was, it made Dun happy. He lumbered toward us. smacking his lips, as Duib attached Mac Tíre.

Síofra covered her mouth to stifle a scream and backed against the ivy-covered wall, fumbling for the entrance.

While she searched, I gripped my torch in both hands like a weapon, as my sword instructor had demonstrated. As Dun lunged toward me, I swung the torch at his head.

Dun yelped and backed away, giving me a wide berth. Gray clouds rolled toward us as though in a hurry to join the fight. Plump raindrops fell from the sky. My torch smoldered. Rain? Really? Speaking of sides—if I needed a message that the Celtic gods were not on our side, this was it. I swung the torch again and it sputtered, creating a trail of smoke.

Dun hesitated, while Cooley and Duib stalked Mac Tíre. When they raised their clubs, he rolled out of their way. Surprised at his speed, they roared and went after him. Before they could land a blow, he sprang to his feet, doubled up his fist and drove it into Duib's jaw. The giant yelped in pain and swung his club at Mac Tíre's head. Mac Tíre ducked, but Cooley was ready. He clipped Mac Tíre on the shoulder and sent him sprawling to the ground. Both advanced, but Mac Tíre was already on his feet.

He was outnumbered, and I wasn't much help. The torch sputtered out.

Dun snickered, raising his club over his head. I gritted my teeth. We were all going to die.

An arrow sped past my shoulder and embedded in Dun's chest. Blood spread in a perfect circle. A dark stain over his mud-colored tunic. The feathers on the shaft were unusual. Instead of dull brown, they looked like they were dipped in gold.

Holding the spent torch like a weapon, I spun around to the direction of the attack, unsure if the archer had meant to hit me and missed. Shadows moved in the dense foliage, each armed with bows.

Dun cried out, "Oh. Oh." and sank to his knees. He glanced over at his brothers before pitching face down in the dirt.

Cooley and Duib paused in horror. Cooley was the first to recover. He shook his fist in the direction of the shadow archers and ordered Duib to fetch his brother. Duib slung Dun over his shoulders, awaiting further commands.

Cooley backed away, pointing his club at Mac Tíre, and shouted. "This is not over."

Chapter Seven

The shadow archers who'd rescued us vanished as suddenly as they'd appeared, leaving us to make our way to Oghy U without them. From the outside, the building resembled a rectangular church: stained glass windows on three sides, thick walls, and semi-circular arches. The massive structure looked more like a Gothic cathedral than a school.

Mac Tíre had instructed us to stay alert, but as we got closer, we didn't need his warning to approach with caution. One look at the condition of the entrance was all it took. The doors were ripped off their hinges. Not an easy task. They were massive, covered in iron, and had taken an ox cart and six men to carry and install. Students were in the process of reattaching them, but the job seemed overwhelming.

Mac Tíre entered the building first, and Síofra and I followed close behind. Síofra muttered that the school was in chaos. That was an understatement. Bookshelves were turned over, and tables and chairs lay scattered and broken over the floor as though a giant had dumped the school upside down and shaken it a few times for good measure before crushing the contents underfoot.

Students were in a panic. Some hid behind the rubble while the younger ones clung to each other, flinching at every sound.

Despite the chaos, I spun around in awe. I'd never

been allowed inside. The room was circular and larger than the castle's Great Hall. There were thirteen oak paneled double doors evenly spaced and so highly polished you could see your reflection. Marble, as white as new snow, covered alcoves and Roman-style pillars.

"Where are the instructors?" I said.

"Asleep," Mac Tíre said, as he motioned for Síofra and me to stay behind while he scouted the area. I moved forward to protest that I could help, but Síofra held me back with a shake of her head. Leave the warrior-stuff to the menfolk, was what I thought was her reasoning. I was about to make a snappy protest when she nodded to an alcove a short distance away.

"Mac Tíre believes what you are about to witness will help you understand," she said. "But we must be very quiet. The young druid, Liam, has challenged goddess Bridget to a game of *Fidchell*."

I gulped and said. "Did you say goddess Bridget, as in a *real* goddess?"

Síofra shushed me and motioned toward a secluded corner of the room. In the eye of the storm-like atmosphere that had destroyed the university, two people sat playing what looked like a game of chess as though nothing had happened.

The game board wasn't square, however, it was round and made from solid glass. Across the surface was a map of the world etched in gold. Positioned on the square grid were miniature ships, complete in every detail. There were painted miniatures of kings, queens, warriors, pirates, knights, bards, druids, horses, wolves, and ravens, as well as mythological creatures I'd read about in stories.

A young man with floor-length white hair watched

his opponent with hawk-like concentration. The girl's skin was pale, like the inside of a sea shell, and her gown as blue as the morning sea. She was about the same age and seemed unfazed by his direct stare as she moved her king forward. The game piece looked a lot like King Henry VIII, complete with wide shoulders and bird-thin legs.

"Goddess Bridget, are you quite sure you want to make that move?" Druid Liam said smoothly. "The world watches."

"We are running out of options. Our Book has been stolen. The longer it remains in our enemies' hands, the more damage is done not only to the Tuatha, but humankind as well."

"People will die." Liam said.

She lifted her narrow shoulders in a shrug. "My dear druid, it is what humans do best. Your move."

The air around them stilled. I wanted to interrupt, ask questions, but their expressions and the way they leaned toward each other, assessing each other's strengths and weaknesses, told me this was no ordinary game.

Without warning, Liam stood, toppling his chair. Miraculously, none of the pieces moved. "There has to be another way. I evoke my right to suspend the game."

She rose in one fluid motion. "Granted. I've stayed too long as it is. There is a boat leaving for the Island of Beg Ara and I must not be late. Beware, young druid. You allow your emotions to cloud your judgment." She spun in a circle, her gown shimmering like pools of liquid silver, and disappeared.

As Liam righted his chair, he glanced over at me as though he knew I was watching him. I couldn't look away. One minute Bridget was there, and the next she'd vanished. The world and its rules were changing faster than I could keep up.

Liam broke the connection with me first. With his attention back on the game, he rested his elbows on the glass table as though nothing had happened.

It registered that Síofra had been talking to me.

"...the young druid keeps to himself," she was saying in a slightly elevated tone, indicating the scene had disturbed her as much as me. "Liam is not very friendly," she continued, "but as I mentioned, it is understandable given his assignment. The game he plays is called *Fidchell*. There are thirteen game boards in all, spread out over the four corners of the world. They represent the gods and goddesses and their domains. Each year at this time a druid is selected. Liam is the youngest druid ever chosen, but it is rumored that he is not pleased."

"Couldn't he turn the position down?" I said.

"Druid Liam had two choices," a deep male voice answered. "Liam could accept the position or accept death."

****

I learned that the person who had spoken was one of the archers who'd rescued us. He had shoulder-length brown hair held in place by dozens of braids, and a chin that narrowed into a point. A jagged scar marred the left side of his face; evidence he'd been in a recent fight.

He spoke to Síofra in a language I couldn't quite place. She touched the wound on his face tentatively. "Finn," she whispered, "you are hurt."

He pressed a kiss in the palm of her hand. "About

time I looked the part of a warrior." A muscle twitched along his jaw line as he smiled and squeezed her hand gently.

Síofra blushed a soft peach shade as she gazed into Finn's eyes, and I knew this was the young man she'd told me about. Finn wore a brave expression for Síofra's benefit. I liked him immediately, but it highlighted the difference between us. He was taking the danger in stride, I was coming apart at the seams, and it probably showed.

"The goddess who is playing *Fidchell* with Liam mentioned she was sailing to Beg Ara," I said, trying to understand what was happening. "I heard my mother talking about the enchanted island to Mary when they thought I wasn't listening. It is one of the many lands of the Sidhe, which they call Forever Young. What do you think it means?"

Síofra and Finn exchanged a troubled glance. Finn motioned to the huddled group of children I'd seen when I'd first arrived. "Strange things have been happening. A few hours ago, they were full-grown men and women. They are here as visiting speakers, representatives of the Tuatha. When the spell took hold, they started growing younger."

"What do you think it means?" I repeated.

Before Finn had a chance to respond, the children started arguing and with a gentle voice, he turned and asked them to settle down.

My mouth dropped open.

Between Finn's shoulder blades sprouted wings the color of maple leaves in autumn. Why hadn't I noticed them before?

My voice strained. "You have wings," I said,

stating the obvious as I reached toward them. I couldn't help myself. Except instead of remaining still, they flexed and twisted out of my reach in the same way a cat's tail moved when you tried to touch it.

As fast as a blink, they vanished. I looked toward Liam to check if he had them as well. If he did, they weren't visible. He was, however, focused on the game. His hand hovered over one of the board pieces, debating his next move.

I'd been at the school a short time and already had more questions than answers. Mary had talked about the castle and its secrets. I wished I'd asked her what she'd meant.

Mac Tíre reappeared with a knapsack slung over his shoulder and capes over his arm. He set his bundles down and withdrew a sword from the scabbard attached to his belt. He swung it a few times, testing its weight. "Borrowed a weapon. Hope you don't mind. And thank you and your shadow archers for rescuing us from the Herding Boys."

Finn gave a slight bow. "We are in this together, friend."

Mac Tíre gave me an uneasy look. "What's with Grace?"

Síofra reached out toward me and gave my hand a gentle squeeze. "She's seeing our world for the first time. She's not prepared."

Mac Tíre's eyebrows knitted together and shook his head. "It's all happened too fast for her." He moved toward me and rested his hand on my shoulder. "Grace, you can take off the ring. You'll remember everything that has happened but at least you won't see goblins, or things like Finn's wings anymore, and we will hide you until this is over."

"Mac Tíre is right," Síofra said. "We are part of this, but you can choose."

I glanced down at the ring on my finger. Mac Tíre had given me a way out. I didn't have to get involved. It was one thing to dream of monsters and things that went bump in the night, another to know they existed. Talking it off seemed like good advice, but my mother had given me the ring. She believed in me. The next step was to believe in myself.

I looked over at Síofra. For all her brave words, she was as afraid as I was. She gripped Finn's arm so tight her knuckles shone as white as sun-bleached bones. She hadn't been surprised by Finn's wings, or the Herding Boys only having one eye, or the tutor assassin. She'd known all along they were real. It made sense now. She always talked about gods and goddesses in the present, not in Ireland's distant past.

In a flash of clarity, I knew the whispers about Síofra being abandoned by her mother were true. She was a Changeling. A child of the Sidhe. This was her fight as much as Finn's. I didn't know yet how Mac Tíre fit in, but Mary thought he was involved somehow. Another thing was also clear: my best friend wasn't taking the easy way out and neither would I. I wouldn't abandon her.

I stepped forward. "I'm staying."

"Then you will die."

Síofra frowned at Mac Tíre. "Must you always say, 'the sky is falling'? Maybe once you could say, 'everything will be all right.' Maybe it is not as bad as we think."

"It's a whole lot worse, and I don't say the sky is

falling unless it's true. Like now. There is strong evidence of Belladonna and traces of an unknown substance. I smelled the same thing on the *Red Branch*. I warned Grace's father, but he wouldn't listen. He said there was no such thing as magic potions and spells. Next thing we knew, we were under attack."

"Any chance someone dressed in long robes was onboard the enemy's ship?" I said, remembering my tutor.

Mac Tíre nodded. "Yes, that was part of the information I shared with your mother. The man appeared when the storm intensified. When he raised his arms, there was an explosion and I was thrown overboard." A muscle hardened along his jaw. "I tried to make it back to the ship, but it had already disappeared."

My throat tightened. I wanted to tell him it wasn't his fault, but he seemed so closed off, I doubted he'd hear me. Instead I said, "My tutor waved his arms and everyone in the castle fell asleep. Do you think it's the same person?"

We all held our breath, no doubt sharing the same paralyzing thought. My father's ship and the attack on the castle and Oghy U were all connected.

"Whoever did this," Finn said, breaking the silence, "knew what they were doing. This is no ordinary sleeping spell. We can't rule out the possibility of poison, but it also appears that anyone over the age of sixteen slips into a deep sleep. An effective way to eliminate seasoned warriors. Did the Femorian tell you how long we have?"

"Until midnight on Samhain Eve," I said.

Finn closed his eyes for a second as though trying

to block out bad news. "Yesterday I overheard Headmaster Mac Elatha arguing with the other instructors. *Lebor Gabála Érenn* was missing and they were worried. If anyone tampers with the Book, tears out pages or removes it from its protective container, time might be altered. It is also known as *The Book of Invasions* and *The Book of the Taking of Ireland*. The name changes, depending on its owner. They should call it *Goblin Poop,* for all the trouble it's caused over the years."

"Does it have gold and silver drawings of horses, ravens and the Goddess Epona?" When everyone nodded, I continued. "John Dee showed it to me this morning. Well, not exactly willingly. It dropped out of his hands when I bumped into him."

Síofra said, "Yesterday, he wanted to talk to me about a book he'd found, but when Grace arrived, he changed his mind. I never saw him again."

Finn rubbed the back of his neck. "That little traitor. We trusted him with our secrets and he repaid us by stealing our history. I knew there was something odd about him. He was obsessed with foretelling the future." Síofra touched his arm and lifted an eyebrow. He shrugged. "Fine. I admit, the Sidhe and their druids like messing with time and dimensions as well, but when he does it, it's creepy."

"And that explains our other problem," Mac Tíre said. "Most of the gods, goddesses, and their champions have disappeared. My guess is, like the goddess, they are headed for *Beg Ara*. They realized the Book was stolen. They are afraid whoever has it will find a way to take away their magical powers. *The Book of Invasions* can rewrite history, change the course of a battle, determine the victor, crown a commoner king, or erase an entire civilization from the face of the earth."

Síofra was staring at the children. "If pages were torn out, that might explain why the Tuathan warriors are becoming younger."

"Just a thought," I said. "Shouldn't a book that powerful be destroyed?"

A battering ram vibrated through the walls, making my point. The students repairing the damaged entrance screamed and backed away. Finn and his shadow archers formed a line, their bows raised, and their arrows notched and aimed at the entrance. The battering ram thundered again. Wood panels cracked as the makeshift doors strained to keep our enemies out and us safe.

A girl with wings that grew darker with each step rushed over to Finn.

"The Fire Lord has arrived."

That did not sound good.

Mac Tíre seemed oblivious to the battering ram and rising tension as he handed Finn a cape. "These should conceal our identity. I packed bread, dried fish, cheese, healing potions, poison, and a Mouldywarp antidote, in case we encounter Fallen Fairies in the underground. They have this nasty habit of paralyzing their victims."

Finn looked agitated. "Mouldywarps are the least of my concern. Didn't you hear Una? Lord Aillén is here. I can't go with you now. I have to stay here and defend the school. If he sets fire to the school…"

"My tutor said his name was Mr. Aillén. But I pushed him to his death."

****

Mac Tíre shot me a quick glance. "Your tutor is the Fire Lord?" He whistled through his teeth. "Lord Aillén breaths fire and enjoys watching things burn. You killed him? That is impressive."

Finn turned pale. "Lord Aillén can't be killed. He is immortal and is supposed to be languishing in the Land of the Dead."

Síofra started pacing to help calm her nerves, a trick she had learned from me. "In our distant past, Lord Aillén burned Tara to the ground every Samhain Eve and no one could stop him." She paused and turned toward me. "Tara is where our kings and queens are crowned, so the gods were annoyed with all the building and rebuilding..." She sighed. "Finally, our champion, Fionn mac Cumhaill, appeared and defeated Lord Aillén with an enchanted spear. Whoever stole the book must have discovered a way to free him."

Mac Tíre snapped a cape around his shoulders. "Magical rules are readjusting, and not in our favor."

Finn cast a nervous glance between the bank of windows and the children. "Lord Aillén can only set fires on October thirty-first, six days from today. But as we've found out, he has acquired sorcerer's powers as well. He is very dangerous." Finn looked like he was going to be sick. "Did I forget to mention that one of the children, the one sucking his thumb, is Fionn mac Cumhaill?"

"Isn't that good news? We can use his enchanted spear and kill Lord Aillén."

Finn shook his head slowly. "He left it with the druid, Mug Ruith, for safekeeping. We have a rule about bringing magical weapons into the school."

Mac Tíre shrugged. "No worries. I'll find John Dee

and the Book. I know where to find Mug Ruith. You hold the school until I return."

"I'm going with you," I blurted, surprised at my boldness. When my breathing slowed, I repeated my announcement to a stunned audience. John Dee was my friend. I didn't want to believe he was a traitor. I wanted to give him a chance to explain his side. I had a feeling Mac Tíre acted first and ask questions later.

"No," both Mac Tíre and Finn said together.

Síofra disentangled her arm from Finn's to stand beside me. "I'm going with Grace."

I mouthed a thank you. "You need us," I said. "John Dee has no reason to suspect we mean him any harm. If he sees Mac Tíre, he'll run. I would."

Mac Tíre raised an eyebrow. "They have a point." His admission sounded strained, as though he rarely spoke those words. Then he added. "I'll keep them safe."

Finn glanced over at Síofra. "You'd better. Grace, didn't you say John Dee claimed he was keeping the Book safe?" When I nodded, he continued. "If he already turned the Book over to the Femorians, we wouldn't be standing here. We'd be dead. No need for a deadline. I believe the Femorians are after him as well. John Dee was an interesting choice to steal the Book. He's unpredictable. The Headmaster even suggested he thought the boy a little mad. You can't rule out the possibility that he is not acting on his own."

I said. "He told me once the stars foretold he'd be a famous sorcerer in England."

"Did he now?" Finn looked like he'd discovered bread. He slapped Mac Tíre on the shoulder. "I know where he's going. If I were as ego-driven as John Dee,

I'd betray the Femorians and head for where I thought my brand of madness would be the most appreciated: England. He'll not risk traveling over the high seas. At least at first. The ocean is the Femorians' domain. Most likely he'll use the underground passage tombs to reach Dublin and the English garrison or seek asylum in Gorias, one of the four cities of Tir na nÓg. I'll send word to the druid, Esras of New Grange, to be on the lookout. You can overtake John Dee by using the Passage Tomb, *Cnoc Meadha*."

"Why is it so quiet?" Mac Tíre raced over to one of the windows. Just as he said it I realized I hadn't heard the battering ram for some time. "Remember when you said the Fire Lord was our biggest problem? Look again."

We all followed Mac Tíre's lead. The battering ram had been pushed to the side. While we were inside, the day had grown darker. Shadows flanked Lord Aillén, swaying in the rain-soaked breeze.

"Lord Aillén brought reinforcements," Finn said. "The shadows you see are called *Marbh Bhee*, the Walking Dead. Whoever is behind this attack timed it perfectly. The portals to the Otherworld are weakest before Halloween. If Lord Donn, or worse, Crom Cruach is behind the Goblin rising…well, let's hope they're not. Food is not the only thing the Walking Dead are allowed to bring back to their realm."

Chapter Eight

Speaking of food, while I waited for Mac Tíre and Síofra, I finished off a small piece of bread and fish at the entrance to the passage tomb, Cnoc Meadha. It wasn't as good as Mary's, and so far, Cnoc Meadha was a disappointment as well.

The passage tomb didn't look like much on the outside. I expected twinkling lights or an entrance guarded by giants, not a raised patch of ground shaped like the top of a person's head. Instead of hair, the mound was covered in tall grass the color of dried straw.

I glanced over my shoulder toward the castle. It was close to midnight and the world was draped in shadows. Mother would have ordered torches, candles, and bonfires to chase away the gloom. But she was asleep, and it was as dark as the inside of a tomb.

Otherworld was exactly what the word implied. The passage tombs didn't just tunnel underground, they lead to portals in the Sidhe realm. These alternate dimensions had been created when the Tuatha lost their battle with the Milesians. Even after all I'd experienced, I was excited to test this theory.

"Stay close to me," Mac Tíre ordered, walking past me.

Síofra hurried to catch up, rolling her eyes at Mac Tíre as she sped by. "You will get used to him."

"I doubt it," I said under my breath.

With Mac Tíre leading the way—again—we entered Cnoc Meadha.

Good news: it was dark.

Bad news: it was dark.

Inside was cold and damp. Two of my least favorite things. A spider skittered over my boot and I flinched. Make that three things I disliked.

We were going down.

Bats covered the roof of the cave and tunnels like a cape made of lumpy black velvet. In the world above, they sailed across the sky as soundlessly as a gentle breeze through the trees. Maybe because they spent so much energy chattering down here, they were calmer when they reached the surface. Whatever the reason, the sound was deafening and that was the real reason no one was talking. We were afraid the bats would notice us and attack.

For some reason, that possibility felt better than the one where we'd just realized we were stuck together on an impossible quest. We all had spent our lives living as outsiders, not quite fitting in. Síofra because the villagers felt she was a Changeling and would bring them bad luck, and me because I never measured up to my parents' expectations. Their dreams and mine would never be the same. Mac Tíre was a mystery, but I felt safe with him for some reason. Which was annoying.

The bats' chattering spiked. The sound was so loud I covered my ears. Then Mac Tíre did the strangest thing. He used his cape to stir up the bats into a mad frenzy. He whipped it back and forth in front of them until they were as agitated as a swarm of angry bees.

Síofra clenched her hands into fists and lifted her

chin to give Mac Tíre a piece of her mind.

He didn't give her the chance.

"We're being followed." He tossed his cape in the direction we'd come.

The bats attacked his cape as though they believed it was a living creature. I didn't rule out the possibility that he had placed a glamour on his cape to make the bats think it was alive.

We raced down a narrow passageway. Our torches bobbled as we ran, casting long shadows over the walls. I worried about Finn and the other student-warriors at Oghy U. They'd stayed behind, giving us time to find the Book. I hoped their confidence in us wasn't misplaced. Finn should have been the one on this quest, not me.

Mac Tíre stopped abruptly. Before us were the entrances to three separate tunnels. "They're getting closer."

"I don't hear anything…"

Screams echoed through the underground tunnels.

"The bats found a new target," Mac Tíre said. "Extinguish the torches. Bats may not be the dumbest on the food chain, but they're close. I knew they'd follow my cape and then turn on whoever got in the way, but we have to hurry. Black Druids are relentless. They never give up."

"Whoa. Black Druids. I thought druids were scholars, not fighters," I said.

"Their focus depends on who they swear allegiance to," Síofra said as she followed Mac Tíre's lead and snuffed out her torch on the dirt floor.

I looked toward the mouth of the tunnels, each one blacker than a cloudless night, and I turned to Síofra for support. "If we extinguish our torches, we can't see where we're going. We could walk off a ledge, into a pit of snakes, spiders…" I shivered, tightening my grip on my torch. I had no intention of snuffing it out. I wasn't exactly afraid of the dark, but I didn't like the thought of something hiding in the shadows waiting to attack. It made me edgy. I'd rather see what it was and meet it face to face.

Mac Tíre uncoiled the rope fastened to his belt and handed me the end. "Hold on." Then he jabbed his finger at my torch. A clear signal I was the only one left who hadn't followed orders. The story of my life.

"So now our hero can see in the dark?" I said, knowing I sounded whiney.

Síofra's lips were pressed together. "He'll have to tell you himself."

With that cryptic answer we plunged deeper into the passage tomb.

****

The farther down we went, the colder it became, but it wasn't pitch-black as I'd thought. The quality of light resembled a typical overcast Irish winter. Even so, the underground made me more and more uneasy. I liked it when the air tasted of salt from the sea, rather than choking dust from caves.

Sticky cobwebs caught in my hair and clung to my face. I swiped at them as a small spider shifted into view.

"You've made her angry," Síofra said to me, as she tried to reattach a strand of the web I'd destroyed. "It took her a month to make her home."

I wanted to say a spider's *home* was a trap for unsuspecting insects and people minding their own business, but one look at Síofra and I changed my mind. I was learning a whole new way of viewing the world. Although most humans believed plucking wings off insects was cruel, if they were caught the most he or she would receive was a lecture. But the Sidhe respected all living things, and what was more, knew that winged creatures weren't always just insects, sometimes they were fairies in disguise. In the cities of the Otherworld, plucking wings off insects resulted in banishment or worse.

Síofra stared at the wisps of silken web in silence. If anything, her expression had saddened. She looked like someone who'd seen a small animal injured.

I whispered an apology and bent over to see if I could help.

"Spiders can't keep secrets," Mac Tíre announced, heading in the direction the spider had skittered. "I'll try to reason with her."

A few days ago, I would have laughed, thinking he was joking. "Who would she tell?" I couldn't believe I'd just said that. I knelt, trying to fix the strands, but they were sticky and kept breaking. I sat back. "The creatures down here are so small they're more of a nuisance than a real threat. Right?"

"Not everything is small," Síofra said. "Mouldywarps are giant moles, the size of long boats."

"Mouldywarps?" I said to Síofra, trying to stay calm.

Síofra concentrated on repairing the web. "Mouldywarps are only one of the forms they take. When a member of the Sidhe breaks our laws, they are considered a fallen fairy, and the Otherworld council has the authority to turn them into something vile.

Usually they choose a mole for obvious reasons. Fairies like being outside. Banishment underground is the worst type of punishment. As a result, they are always in a bad mood. That is why moles ruin gardens. They are not happy about being forced to live where it is dark all the time. They retaliate by destroying anything of beauty."

"But moles eat worms. Maybe they'll leave us alone."

Mac Tíre returned, dusting off his knees. "That was a waste of time. Cornella would not listen to reason. Hopefully, she'll forget. Spiders have short memories. Did you tell Grace that Mouldywarps only eat worms if they cannot find people or fairies?"

I felt like someone had thrown water in my face. Ice-cold water.

After that revelation, we continued in silence, locked in our own thoughts, which at least in my case wasn't such a good idea. Without conversation as a distraction, I heard everything around me. The flapping of wings I hoped belonged to fairies, the good kind, not the fallen kind. Squeaking sounds that were either bats or rats. Probably both. Then there was the occasional slither associated with snakes. If you'd heard St. Patrick banished all the snakes in Ireland, you were misinformed. They went underground.

A roar vibrated around us, spreading clouds of choking dust through the air. Underground, with low visibility, I couldn't tell where the sound came from, much less what it was.

Then Mac Tíre pointed behind me. "Mouldywarp."

The biggest mole I'd ever seen in my life took up the entire width and height of the passageway. Covered in mud-brown fur, he had a long pink nose, small eyes and ears, and human-like hands. It opened its mouth and licked its lips.

We all screamed at the same time and ran.

****

We reached a dead end.

Cautiously, we entered the circular room. Illuminated as though by moonlight, exposed tree roots covered in moss twisted down rock walls. Leaves sprouted from the wood and turned their faces toward the ceiling, while a flat stone slab, about waist high, rested in the center of the chamber.

"I think we lost him," Síofra said, catching her breath.

Mac Tíre dumped his knapsack on the slab. He didn't look relieved. He looked worried. He kept glancing in the direction we'd come.

Síofra spun around. "Do you know what this is?"

"A big rock?" I offered.

Síofra shook her head slowly as she spread her fingers over the Celtic swirls and dashes etched over the surface. "I'm referring to the designs. They are called Ogham, the ancient tree language, named for Oghma, the God of Writing. The school is named after him."

"I knew that."

Mac Tíre ran his hand over the symbols with the same reverence. "Oghma wanted a way to help the Tuatha and Femorians communicate. Some even believe the symbols he designed had power. Although he was Femorian, his wife, Etan, was Tuathan. The peace didn't last long."

They were lost in the memory of ancient deities.

67

All great stuff. Unless the distraction made you forget you were hunted by giant people-eating mole monsters. Then, not so much.

I heard the crash, and then a low growl. The Mouldywarp had picked up our scent.

Mac Tíre drew his sword.

"Any ideas?" I said.

Mac Tíre narrowed his gaze and stared over my shoulder. "Are the walls moving?"

Pouring out of cracks and crevices like boiling water over the rim of an iron pot were thousands and thousands of angry spiders. Obviously, Cornella had a better memory than most spiders and had brought her friends. They swarmed over the ground in angry, black waves, heading straight toward us.

"Quick," Mac Tíre said. "Climb onto the Ogham Stone."

We scrambled up just as the spiders reached the edges of the slab.

"The Oghma's symbols will protect us," Mac Tíre said, but he didn't sound convinced.

We formed a tight circle.

"Are they poisonous?" I said.

No one answered.

I jabbed Mac Tíre in the ribs.

He glared at me. "Cornella didn't say. She was too busy screaming at me."

****

I wasn't sure how long we'd been standing on the Ogham Stone, but the light in the chamber seemed brighter somehow. Fear had a way of distorting reality, I reasoned. Plus, my legs ached and our ideas for escaping bordered on the absurd. When Mac Tíre offered to marry Cornella, I knew the end was near.

The spiders seemed hesitant to climb the slab. They swirled around us, with no sign of growing tired. "They aren't interested in harming us," I said. "Their job is to keep us here until the Mouldywarp arrives. My guess is that he is busy hunting. Or eating."

Mac Tíre and Síofra nodded agreement. I tried to remember how to breathe. I thought of all the times my mother tried to get rid of moles. They ruined her garden and made big holes where flowers had been. It was the only time I'd ever heard her say a bad word. Just last week, she'd said she'd solved the mole problem. I'd never asked her how. I wished I'd paid better attention.

The room grew brighter as though the sun had risen.

Birds chirped happily overhead.

It took a moment to register.

We all looked toward the ceiling at the same time. Clouds drifted overhead, clearly visible through a covering of a green gauze-like substance. I hadn't noticed it before. I'd just assumed the top of the cave was solid rock.

"It's a mushroom veil," Síofra whispered in awe. "I've never seen it from this angle. They are the center of a fairy ring. From the surface they resemble solid ground. Anyone who steps into the middle of the ring falls into the realm of the Sidhe."

Hope flickered.

"Mac Tíre, you're the tallest," I said. "You go first, and then pull the rest of us through. Or Síofra and I can stand on your shoulders." Síofra and Mac Tíre exchanged glances. Why were they hesitating?

Síofra spoke slowly as though weighing each word.

"Fairy rings are unpredictable. There are those who believe they are living, breathing entities. I've never heard of anyone going back through a fairy ring, only dropping down the center of one. The only way I know to leave the Otherworld is through the passage tombs." She slid Mac Tíre another glance. "And then there's the part about a curse."

"That is only a legend," he said, but he didn't sound convinced.

I glanced toward the veil with growing unease. "How about you tell me about the legend? I like that word better than *curse*."

Síofra looked as uneasy as I felt as she focused on the veil as though it were exactly what she'd said: a living, breathing entity. "According to legend, the Tuatha were angry with humans. They blamed them for either neglecting or tearing down the Sidhe's honored sites and twisting their stories by turning benevolent gods into demons. At the same time, humans continued to visit the magical realms, even marrying members of the Sidhe and having their children. In retaliation, the Sidhe placed a curse on all fairy rings. Humans can fall through, but once inside, no one with even a drop of human blood can return to the surface the way they came."

I put my hand on her shoulder. "That's why you always placed small rocks around the fairy rings. You were afraid the curse was real."

A low snarling noise filled the alcove.

Legend or reality, we'd run out of options.

Mac Tíre leapt through the veil and grabbed the edge. In a matter of seconds, he had scrambled to solid ground. He reached through the veil toward us. "Give me your hands," he shouted.

I pushed Síofra forward. She shook her head, giving me an odd look. "You first."

"I'm right behind you."

Mac Tíre pulled Síofra through then reached for me.

I stretched up and we locked hands. He pulled me toward the veil as he had Síofra moments before. The Mouldywarp's snarl became a growl so fierce it scattered the spiders. My heart raced so loud it rang in my ears. This had to work.

When the tips of my fingers touched the veil, the consistency turned as solid as glass. He pulled again, smashing my fingers again the surface, breaking our grip. I dropped back down, rubbing my fingers. "Why didn't it work?" I yelled.

"It is the curse," Síofra shouted with rising panic. Her voice was muffled and seemed far away. "What are we going to do?"

"I'll go back." Mac Tíre jumped into the center; the veil vibrated but remained solid. He looked confused. "What happened? What's stopping me?"

Síofra's eyes brimmed with tears. "It's my fault. I should have known. The curse won't let us rescue Grace."

The Mouldywarp appeared in the entrance of the cave. This time his growling noises sounded more like laughter than a roar.

Chapter Nine

The Mouldywarp was big and furry, and his eyes were so small they were almost invisible. What sent cold shivers through me were his hands. They were long, and bony, and each fingernail looked as sharp as the blade of a sword. I tried to keep my expression blank as my mother had advised. She taught me the technique. Behave like the legendary Gray Man, she would say, whenever faced with an unknown or dangerous situation. Don't react. Don't show emotion. Assess your situation and plan your escape.

Above me, my friends yelled and stomped on the veil. The Mouldywarp was unfazed as he ambled forward. I stepped back, balancing on the edge of the Ogham Stone. The place was a dead end with nowhere to hide and the monster blocked the only escape route.

He swept the back of his paw against my side as though swatting a fly. I sailed across the room. The force knocked me against the wall. Spiders scattered. I scrambled to my feet, ignoring the throbbing pain in my back, more afraid than ever. If he'd meant to kill me, I'd be dead. The thought wasn't comforting.

My friend's muffled shouting finally caught his attention. He lifted his snout as though sniffing the air. Directly above him was the mushroom veil.

"Mac Tíre's knapsack," Síofra voice sounded far away. "There's a bottle of poison," she screamed.

"Throw it at the Mouldywarp. It might slow him down. There's also an antidote if he…"

Mac Tíre balled his fist and punched the veil. It held. His knuckles bleeding, he punched again. A wave-like current moved over the surface, holding the Mouldywarp's attention. While he made silly mole faces at my friends, I snatched the discarded knapsack from under his nose. Inside were vials in all shapes, sizes, and colors imaginable. Which one was the antidote and which one the poison?

I stood, waving my arms to get Síofra's attention.

I also drew the Mouldywarp's interest. He drew back his paw, but instead of striking me, he waved his paw in the direction of the mushroom veil. In a flash of light, the mushroom veil closed. I couldn't see my friends or the world above. The use of magic stunned me for a moment until I remembered—he was not just a very large mole but one of the Fallen Fairies.

The Mouldywarp snorted and turned his attention on me again. From what I knew about these creatures, they were masters at building underground tunnels with their powerful arms and hands. But they weren't known for speed. If I could distract him, slow him down, I might have a chance.

He reached back to take another swipe. I was ready. I palmed a rock, rushed forward, and slammed it on his paw.

The squeal was so loud the noise vibrated against the walls and ceiling, and rocks and twigs rained down like hail. He stuffed his injured paw in his mouth, like a child, and glared at me.

I hit him on the other paw.

He flinched in pain, but kept his beady eyes

focused on me. I feigned to the left. He anticipated the move and blocked my path. His expression turned cruel, almost human. Playtime was over. If I could read his thoughts, I was pretty sure it would be something like: *Time to neutralize this annoying creature.*

I hugged the wall and edged toward the exit. His tongue snaked out of his mouth. Green goop dripped to the ground in puddles that sizzled and smoked. The few remaining spiders making their escape were caught in the goo. I hoped Cornella wasn't among them. I didn't harbor any ill will, as she had only wanted to defend her home.

The Mouldywarp's tongue snaked out again. I ducked but not in time. It slathered me in a coating of drool from my neck to the tips of my toes. Burning pain seared through every nerve in my body so intensely it hurt to breathe. My arms were plastered to my sides and my legs felt as though they were taking root in the ground.

The Mouldywarp smacked his lips for what seemed the hundredth time. He looked pleased with himself. I wanted to wipe the expression off his ugly face, but it was growing harder and harder to move.

He crouched in front of me as though he were waiting for something. My breath was ragged. My lungs felt like they were being crushed by an invisible hand. If this giant mole thought I would wait for a second bath of goop, he was delusional.

I managed to wiggle one of my arms free, but the knapsack was too far away. Taking short, shuffling steps, I moved toward it, hoping I'd find the poison in time. The Mouldywarp watched, as though amused at what he probably thought was my attempt at escape.

With any luck, Mac Tíre had marked the poison vile with a skull and crossbones design.

The Mouldywarp let loose another round of green goop. I tried to move. This time even my fingers weren't working. My thoughts ordered my body into action. Nothing responded.

I remembered something my mother had told me about moles when I was helping her with the gardening. Their saliva was a type of poison, capable of paralyzing worms. With the worms unable to move, the mole would take them to his cave to snack on later. My stomach turned.

I glanced over at the Mouldywarp, convinced I saw him smile.

****

The Mouldywarp carried me slung over his shoulder through a maze of tunnels that all looked the same. When he stopped, the smell was the first thing to register. A mixture of month-old potato peels, egg shells, and rotting leaves.

He stacked me against a wall as though he had all the time in the world. Which, of course, he did. Light was coming from somewhere, but I couldn't tell where. All I knew was that I was covered with a thin film of green yuck. He sniffed my face, then lumbered through the entrance to a tunnel on the opposite side of the room.

I gulped in the foul-smelling air, taking in my surroundings. If I was going to escape, and I wouldn't allow myself to think of any other scenario, I needed to evaluate my options.

At first glance, the chamber resembled the root cellar beneath my parents' castle. We stored nuts, apples, grains, and potatoes in wooden barrels or on shelves. Ropes of garlic and bunches of dried herbs hung from the rafters. A well-stocked root cellar was a source of pride and meant the difference between survival and starvation over long winter months or in the case of an enemy siege. This particular root cellar, however, smelled like death.

I shuddered. The Mouldywarp had the same survival plan as my parents. He just had a different concept of food. There were skinny, fat, and king-size worms. Worms with bulging eyes and worms that looked sound asleep. If I weren't paralyzed, I would've retched up my breakfast.

"You're not a worm."

The voice sounded close.

I blinked, thinking at first one of the worms had spoken. Anything was possible. Then a young man about my age moved into my line of vision. Mac Tíre's knapsack was slung over his shoulder and he held a bucket in one hand and a knife in the other. He wore a hooded cape, clasped together by a gold pendant.

When I tried to speak, nothing happened. My vocal cords were as frozen as the rest of me. Evidently, the Mouldywarp didn't like his food screaming.

The boy gazed at me as though trying to figure out who or what I was. "You're a human girl," he announced with a satisfied grin. He looked pleased with himself, as though he'd figured out how long it would take to sail around the world. "My name's Angus." He said it proudly as though I should know who he was. "You shouldn't be here. The Mouldywarp will eat you."

My first thought: *You think*? Under any other circumstances, I might have rolled my eyes. Instead I mouthed the word help.

He glanced in the direction where I'd last seen mole-guy. "I'm not supposed to help your kind. Father will be unhappy." He grinned. "Bonus." He grabbed his bucket and tossed the contents over me.

Ice-cold water hit me in the face. I sucked in my breath. The cold sensation turned to heat. It felt like one minute I'd plunged into a freezing lake and the next I stood too close to a blazing fire. All the while my body glowed with pin-pricks of shimmering blue lights.

When they changed to a rosy-pink there was no more discomfort, only a warm sensation as though I were back home in my own room, safe and protected. I swayed on my feet as my eyelids grew sleepy.

He shook me awake. "Run now. Sleep later."

"The water… It… I'm… I'm no longer paralyzed. So sleepy."

"Side effect. Doesn't last. The water heals, but I discovered it also thinks neutralizing the Mouldywarp's venom qualifies. Not sure why."

I had reached for the side of the cave, determined to keep my balance, when his words sank in. "Water that thinks?"

"And refills its container."

What he was talking about sounded like stories I'd heard about the Cauldron of Plenty. Water that healed warriors. True to his word, the bucket filled to the brim.

"Where'd it come from?"

"I sort of borrowed it from my father."

"But that would mean you are one of Dagda's sons. He's known as the Good God."

Angus frowned. "He paid a bard to say that." He glanced over his shoulder. "The Mouldywarp returns."

"We can't outrun it," I said, stating the obvious. Even if my legs weren't still wobbly, I remembered what had happened the last time. Outrunning this monster was not an option. I thought of Finn. Maybe we could fly out of here," I said. "I don't suppose you have wings."

He frowned as though the thought were distasteful. "One of my half-brothers does. I haven't seen him for a while. Even if he were here, I doubt he'd help me. My family and I aren't on speaking terms. They don't approve since I..." His voice trailed off. "We need a diversion."

I glanced over at the rows and rows of paralyzed worms and wondered if they were as frustrated as I was about what had happened to them. "I have an idea. Hand me your bucket."

Angus guessed my plan and nodded approval. He produced another container and divided the water between us.

I headed for the shelves where the worms were stacked one on top of the other. Their eyes were open and staring at me, probably in the same way I'd looked at Angus. I had to admit I'd never given them a thought one way or another before unless it was to cringe.

Right now, we had a mutual enemy. Besides, Mother had said worms were good for the garden as opposed to moles that, simply put, were not. I had a newfound respect for worms. They deserved a fighting chance.

I tossed the water over the worms on the shelves first, silently telling them that this was for my mother. Angus was doing the same thing on the other side of the room. Our containers refilled seconds after they'd emptied. We tossed water over those hanging from the ceiling or propped against the walls. They revived faster than I had, and I had the distinct impression they were grateful.

Angus tapped me on the shoulder and nodded toward the entrance. The Mouldywarp had returned. His eyes narrowed into black slits. He didn't look happy that I'd freed his food. His anger turned to shock when the worms attacked.

We ran for our lives.

Chapter Ten

We burst into a light so bright I expected to see a thousand or more lit candles. I raised my arm to shield my eyes until they adjusted.

The air smelled fresher than in the underground tunnels, but it still seemed stagnant. I missed the ocean and the salt sea breezes. Meadows spread out toward the horizon while birds the size of warships soared overhead. The only flaws were a bank of gray clouds moving from the south and a few wilted flowers.

"Where are we?"

"Tir na nÓg, The Land of Forever Young," Angus said and handed me Mac Tíre's knapsack. "This might come in handy." He gazed over the landscape. "This is as far as I'm allowed to go. Promise me you won't tell anyone I rescued you."

"I don't like keeping secrets."

"Me either, but remember, whatever you say here will be overheard," he paused. "I have a lot of enemies. Many are looking for me and want me dead." Suddenly, he gazed past me. "Your friends are here. They must have entered through another fairy ring."

I looked away for a second and when I turned back, he'd disappeared.

"There she is," I heard Síofra say.

Mac Tíre and Síofra rushed toward me, both grinning as though they'd thought they'd never see me again. Mac Tíre quickly snuffed out his smile but Síofra looked like she did when Mary made her famous almond butter cake.

Síofra squished me in a hug. "I told Mac Tíre you didn't need saving, although we were planning the best rescue ever."

"I told you the vials of poison and antidotes would come in handy," Mac Tíre said, retrieving the knapsack and looking inside. He lifted his head, puzzled. "You did not use them."

"I…I didn't need them." I glanced over my shoulder, hoping Angus would reappear so I could give him credit. I wanted to tell my friends what really had happened, but what if Angus was right? I didn't know what trouble he was in or who wanted him dead, but I had a feeling it had to do with his father and the magic water.

"If the reunion is over, we need to keep moving." A young man stood on the edge of the wood in a suit of armor. Instead of a sword, there was a slingshot looped over his belt.

Síofra crossed her arms over her chest, unfazed by his unfriendly expression. "Before we go another step, Lugh of the Long Arm, I want you to tell us why the plants are dying."

He looked confused, as though he didn't understand the question.

Mac Tíre glanced toward the sky. "Really, Síofra? We've been waiting here for hours, shouting for help, and that's your question? How about 'where has everyone gone,' or 'why are there red dragons?' Dragons never leave England or Wales unless it's to launch an attack."

"Dragons?" All thoughts fled as I followed Mac Tíre's gaze. Sure enough, what I'd first thought were really big birds were the most magical creatures I'd ever seen. They soared overhead in colors that ranged from fiery red to deepest amber.

Síofra wound her arm around mine. "Promise not to freak out?"

"In the past two days, I've learned that my father's ship was captured, my castle and the school were placed under a sleeping spell, I was attacked by a one-eyed assassin, the Herding Boys, and a giant, human-eating mole, plus learned that every magical creature I'd ever heard about was real. Trust me, I will not freak out."

"She makes a good point," Mac Tíre said, nodding. "You should start with…"

"I have this," Síofra said. "We are in one of the four cities of Tir na nÓg, nicknamed The Land of Forever Young. When a member of the Sidhe reaches adulthood, they have the option of never growing any older." She glanced over at Lugh. "Except Lugh looks like he is growing younger. How is that possible?"

A woman emerged from a path, dressed in the snow-white robes of a druidess, her blond-white hair skimming the ground. "Your concerns are shared by us all, Síofra."

The woman laced her hands together like interlocking Celtic designs, reminding me of my mother. I stood straighter, trying not to let the sad memory take over. My mother was in a deep sleep and unless we found the Book, she'd never wake up.

When she glanced toward Lugh, her eyes crinkled with worry lines. "Síofra is correct. Lugh, you look younger today than you did yesterday."

"I share your concern," Lugh said. "All the Red Branch champions, Cuchulain, MacCool, and the rest are affected as well. Anyone who is mentioned in the Book of Invasions is at risk. That's why they fled with the gods and goddess to Beg Ara."

"And yet you stayed." I said.

"Running away won't stop the evil from spreading," Lugh said.

"I hate to interrupt," Mac Tíre said, "but we're here for Fionn mac Cumhaill's magic spear. We have a Fire Lord to kill."

"Mug Ruith would never agree to give it to you," said the druidess. "It is safer here."

Lugh rested his hand on his slingshot. "I agree. Lord Aillén is a minor problem. If Balor of the Evil Eye is involved, you'll need me to defeat him, that is, if I'm still old and strong enough to wield a weapon when the time comes. Druid Biróg, you need to leave. If Balor has found a way to return, you will be among the first to feel his wrath."

The druidess shrugged. "Your grandfather has more important things to do than worry about how to kill me. We're being rude. Introduce me to these young people."

I wasn't sure how Lugh knew us well enough to make the introductions, but Mac Tíre and Síofra reacted as though he were the natural choice. I followed their lead.

"Goddess Biróg," Lugh said with the flourish of a courtier. "I'd like to introduce you to Grace, Síofra, and Mac Tíre."

"Biróg saved Lugh's life," Mac Tíre said, "and to

keep him out of danger, he was fostered by Manannan, the God of the Sea."

"Not my favorite god," Síofra added under her breath.

"Yes, little Changeling, I have issues with him as well, but on this occasion he helped Lugh and for that I'm grateful. My regret is not being there in time to rescue Lugh's other two brothers, the poor wee lads."

"You did what you could," Lugh said, "and risked your life. Balor ordered your death when he learned what you'd done."

An old Irish legend edged its way into my thoughts. "If Balor is your grandfather, then your mother is Eithne and your father is Cian Mac Ciancecht. On the advice of a wizard, your grandfather locked his daughter, Eithne, away in a tower with only women to watch over her."

Biróg smiled softly. "But love prevailed. Lugh's father, Cian, rescued Eithne. He noticed her standing by the tower window one day while he was out hunting and fell in love with her at first sight. They married in secret, and when Eithne gave birth to three beautiful boys, Balor was in a rage. He sent one of his mercenaries to capture and drown them. I arrived in time only to save Lugh. His brothers were already dead."

"But why did Balor want to kill his own grandsons?" I said.

Lugh shook his head. "For some reason I cannot remember. My memory fades as I grow younger. All I do remember is that I'm responsible for my grandfather's death. Worse. If he is behind what is happening, I might be the only one to stop him."

****

Bíróg didn't challenge Lugh's assessment; instead she motioned for us to follow her. "Come, children, we have a way to go. I regret that when the Red Branch warriors left, they took all their chariots with them. While we walk, I'll fill you in as best I can. Lugh is not the only one with gaps in memory," Bíróg said as she slipped her hands into her sleeves. "It's the Book. The longer it is separated from its protective container, time and history not only changes, it is erased. Lugh's lack of memory supports that theory. He is moving backward in time, before Nuada of the Silver Arm took over kingship from the cruel Femorian King Bres and turned our world into chaos, making the Tuathans slaves."

"What do Bridget, our mother goddess Danu, and their sister Cally Berry suggest?" Síofra said. "They must have a plan."

"If they do, the triple goddesses have not shared it with me. The War Goddesses of the Morrigan are also silent. If a solution is not found soon, a dark force will spread over the world unchecked, more destructive than the Black Death. It is whispered this is the start of the Goblin Rising." A shadow crossed over her expression. She wrung her hands together. "We must hurry. Mug Ruith is expecting us."

"He is a druid and a Firbolg," Mac Tíre said. "Not comforting. Firbolgs were some of the earliest settlers of Ireland. Their lands were confiscated, and they were forced to live on remote islands. They blame both Femorians as well as the Tuatha. Do you really think they will help us? If Armageddon is marching toward us, how can we trust Mug Ruith will be on our side?"

Biróg pursed her lips. "We don't have a choice. You said it yourself. The Firbolgs were here before the Tuatha and the Femorians. The Femorians can't risk destroying pages where the Firbolgs are mentioned without risk to themselves. Mug Ruith has assured me his people support us."

Mac Tíre gave a curt nod to the sky. "You still haven't explained the Red Dragons."

She sighed. "I've asked them to stay out of sight. I'll speak with them again. Their presence frightens the unicorns."

"With good reason," Mac Tíre nodded. "Why are they even here?"

Biróg looked toward the sky, her expression as worried as Mac Tíre's. "We knew something was wrong even before the Book's disappearance was brought to our attention. Magical creatures from the far reaches of the world began showing up, seeking asylum, as though answering a call. As children of Danu, abandoning those who asked for our help was unthinkable. Quickly, we realized that whoever was behind the summons realized how we would react and created this distraction. We were so busy helping assimilate all the magical beings, we missed the warning signs."

Síofra asked. "Like the plants and trees dying?"

Biróg nodded. "Exactly. Not all magical creatures get along, which only added to the confusion. Imagine putting a fairy in a pool filled with Nucklelavees." I must have given her a blank stare, as she paused and nodded toward me. "The Nucklelavees are from Scotland. They are a type of water horse with flippers for legs and one eye that oozes black slime. They like eating fairies. Nasty creatures. They caused a lot of confusion and distress before they were captured and placed in underwater cages. Thankfully, none of our fairies were harmed.

"After the Nucklelavee," she continued, "we'd learned our lesson. When the Teugghia and her sisters arrived from France, our intake interviews were more thorough. Teugghia marry mortal men and then kill them in their sleep. When they refused to change their ways and abide by our rules, they were, of course, sent packing. The Red Dragons, on the other hand, are our biggest success story. They committed to helping us when we discovered that the Red Branch knights had…"

"Deserted us." Mac Tíre finished.

She looked sad but didn't disagree. She continued her description on the challenges they faced with the increased magical creature infestation. But the tension grew. Mac Tíre had voiced what we were all thinking. How far would the Femorians go to gain control?

An invasion from Ireland's enemies in England, France, and Spain seemed tame compared to flying dragons, fallen fairies, flesh eating water horses, and being overrun by Femorians. I knew the way I looked at the world would never be the same again. The farther along the path Biróg led us, the clearer my vision grew, as though a veil were lifting from my eyes, just as my mother had predicted.

People no taller than my waist peered at me from around fallen tree stumps or tall grasses. They carried babies or held their children's hands and looked as curious about me as I was about them. A mermaid sunned herself on a rock in the middle of a lake that sparkled as though made from liquid crystals. What looked like miniature candle flames danced through the trees and floated in the air above us.

Síofra told me the lights were flower fairies as calmly as though she were naming a variety of rose. Their wings were as transparent as a butterfly's and looked as delicate. Unspoken between us was the fear that these magical beings wouldn't survive in a world of evil and hatred.

When we reached the end of the path, Biróg spread her arms in a wide arc. The trees shimmered a few times and then disappeared, revealing a road wide enough for a coach and six horses to drive through. At the end stood a castle that shone like the inside of an oyster shell, in shades of luminescent pink and pale peach. Tall peaked towers disappeared into the glittering clouds while flags in all the hues of the rainbow fluttered in the breeze. A moat flowed beneath the bridge and circled the castle, while creatures covered in red fur with beady eyes and hawk-like noses clustered together along the shore.

"They're Grogochs," Biróg announced, as though reading my thoughts.

As I watched, two of them popped out of sight. One minute they were there, and in the next, they were gone.

"They are very shy," she explained, "and for the most part keep to themselves. They've never been known to harm anyone, human or magical. If they get nervous, they turn invisible." She arched an eyebrow in warning. "They are, however, fond of creating mischief, so it's always wise to give them food when they ask."

Standing guard was a dragon. He was burnt-yellow and reminded me of a giant sunflower. As I walked over the drawbridge, his gaze didn't leave mine. It was a little unsettling.

"Your dragon doesn't look very happy," I said.

"Would you be if you were forced to exist in a strange form? He arrived with the first wave of immigrants; claimed he was a prince from a small European country and lived in a golden palace. Of course, all enchanted creatures spin a variation of that tale. Their memory seems to melt as fast as a snowflake in July when we ask for details. Even so, and in case he is telling the truth, Mug Ruith continues to experiment with new formulas to try and break his curse. So far, nothing has worked. One of the side-effects is that the dragon's scales change color. Mug Ruith must have tried another potion. This morning, the dragon was a lovely shade of sky blue."

"Do you think I could talk to him?" I said.

"Are you fireproof?"

Chapter Eleven

Biróg, Lugh, Síofra, and Mac Tíre were off to the side—arguing. Mac Tíre wanted Fionn mac Cumhaill's spear but Biróg and Lugh disagreed. All of them were concerned about how to approach Mug Ruith on the topic of the Book's disappearance. Their whispered conversation made me feel like an outsider, and I decided to make myself scarce.

Biróg was an important druidess, Lugh would grow up to be king, Síofra's mother was a member of the Sidhe, and although I wasn't sure who or what Mac Tíre was, it was obvious he wasn't "ordinary" like me.

I settled down on a bench that overlooked the moat, an equal distance between my friends and the dragon. Biróg's "fire proof" comment made me re-think going over to the dragon. I was determined not to fall into a pity party, but my inner annoying voice whispered, *too late*.

Even in my own home, I'd felt like I didn't fit in. As though if I stood in the center of the courtyard and screamed as loud as I could, no one would hear. That whole expression that if a tree fell in the forest, would it make a sound, missed the point. Birds flew out of the way. Animals ran for cover. But did anyone return to see if the tree could have been saved?

A Grogoch popped into view, standing so close I could smell its breath. Lavender with a pinch of thyme.

Then as fast as you could say *why lavender*, another appeared, and another, and another, until there were over a dozen furry creatures no taller than my shoulders with hopeful, wide-eyed stares. I sat up straighter, remembering Bíróg's warning.

Mac Tíre had divided our rations between us and I wasn't sure how he felt about sharing with strangers since the food had to last us until we reached the coast. My stomach grumbled at the mere mention of food, suggesting perhaps I should be the one begging for something to eat. I pressed my hand against my stomach, trying to quiet it down. I hadn't eaten since grabbing a few bits of fish and bread. Did no one but Mouldywarps and Grogochs eat in the Otherworld?

The Grogochs all mirrored my actions, rubbing their hands against their stomachs and moaning for good measure. *I guess the way to express hunger is universal.* Their expressions were so childlike, I melted.

I didn't have much, but I reached into the medicine and herb pouch Mary had packed for me. The pie-crust treats were in crumbs, but still fresh. I divided the bits and pieces into each Grogoch's out-stretched hand and they all made *yum* sounds as I smiled and licked my fingers.

The Grogochs faces then scrunched in frowns and they started chattering to each other at once. I couldn't understand a word they said. Their language reminded me of the sound pebbles made falling into water: all plops and splashes. The Grogochs stopped chattering as abruptly as they'd begun and pointed toward the dragon.

I followed their gaze, thinking maybe he'd changed colors again, when a Grogoch pulled me to my feet.

They crowded around, herding me toward the dragon in the same way dogs herded sheep. It was annoying. No wonder our sheep bleated in protest.

The Grogochs pointed, nodded, and pushed me forward until I was only a few feet from the dragon. His back toward me, he slowly turned his massive head. His gaze moved over me as though I were something he wanted to squish. Or torch.

I tried to back away, but the Grogochs held me in place. Nervous, I said the only thing I could think of to say.

"Were you really a prince?" In my defense, this was my first dragon encounter.

His nostrils flared, smoke snorted out his nose, and he grunted something that sounded a lot like "leave me alone," but I'd caught the expression in his eyes and it stopped me cold. I knew that look. He was in pain, and it didn't take a mind reader to determine the cause.

A sword protruded from his claw-like foot. Emeralds were encrusted in the sword's pommel and gold bands encircled the hilt and cross guard. A weapon worthy of a king or queen, but no less deadly for all its beauty. The dragon's expression reminded me of how one of our wolfhound puppies had reacted when he'd tangled with a thorny rose bush. The rose bush had won.

"Who did this to you?"

His massive shoulders hunched forward, and he looked over at me as though weighing whether or not I'd made fun of him. "It was my fault. I forgot about your traditions. Celts toss their weapons into bogs, lakes, and rivers in tribute to their gods and goddesses. As though Danu and Dagda would want a rusty old blade after it was thrown away. This one's hilt was lodged between rocks with the blade sticking straight up. I didn't see it until it was too late. Mug Ruith said it's called the Sword of *Foghlaí Muir.*"

"The sword has a name?" And then I realized I didn't know the dragon's name. "My name is Grace. What is yours?"

His large mouth turned at the corner in a smile. "How kind of you to ask. My name is William."

Knowing his name made him seem less scary. I moved in a little closer. "Can you tell me why the sword has a name?"

He sighed. "All champion weapons have names. *Foghlaí Muir* means Sea Pirate, in Irish." He gave a very human-like harrumph. "When I first arrived in Ireland, I was filthy and smelly from my long flight, so I took a swim. Seemed like the civilized thing to do before I presented myself to the Tuatha. Imagine my surprise when I stepped on a sword. Whoever created the foolish tradition of discarding weapons in such a manner should be thrown into a bog packed with sharp objects and see how they like it."

I had to agree, only I doubted it was as bad as he said. When I wasn't in the ocean, I spent most of my summers swimming in lakes and rivers. Maybe I had been lucky.

I edged closer and as I did, the Grogochs shuffled with me. I glared at them, but they only smiled up at me encouragingly. "Why haven't you asked someone to help you remove it?"

He hung his head. The expression in his eyes was an odd combination of pain and regret. "It's one of the numerous conditions of my enchantment. If I'm injured, I can't ask for help."

"Well, that's stupid." I hesitated. "Not the people-trying-to-help part, but the can't-ask part."

"Indeed."

Like my puppy, William was suffering. Sure, I still had the scar where the dog had bitten me while I was pulling out the thorns, but he'd drowned me in apology kisses after it was over, and all was forgiven. We were friends for life.

But William wasn't a puppy. He was a dragon. And as calm as he looked and sounded right now, I worried that if I messed this up and managed to drive the blade farther in instead of pulling it out…

I rubbed the scar on my hand, wondering if I really wanted to risk it. Then I made the mistake of looking at William. He looked so sad—just like my puppy—that I said a silent prayer. "Hold still. This might hurt. Oh, and don't set me on fire."

"About that…I should warn you…"

The Grogochs all chattered at once, drowning out the dragon and nudging me in the back.

I got the message. Before I could rethink my decision, I grabbed the hilt of the sword with both hands. William moaned and pressed his jaws together as though he didn't want to accidently set me on fire, which I appreciated. Staring at long, sharp teeth did nothing to calm my nerves. But his reaction also proved that he was in a lot more pain than he'd admitted.

I pulled until my muscles quivered from the strain. The sword didn't budge. It remained as rigid as though it were embedded in stone.

Hoping the Grogochs might help, I turned toward them, but they all stepped back at the same time. One by one, they popped out of sight. Swell. I was on my own.

I tightened my grip. The sword felt warm to the touch as though it had lain too close to a fire. Heat sped up my arms. My hands burned as though I'd grabbed hold of an iron fireplace poker by the wrong end. One look at William's expression and I knew there was no turning back. He hadn't asked for my help and that meant I couldn't give up.

For some reason, the Grogochs and the dragon believed in me and that gave me courage and renewed strength. Ignoring the rising heat radiating from the blade, I flexed my fingers and wound them around the hilt again. Needing leverage, I positioned my foot on the edge of William's paw and pulled.

The blade started to move. I gripped tighter, held my breath, gritted my teeth, and pulled with all my strength.

The weapon slipped free in a hiss of hot steam. The force propelled me backward onto the ground. I slid a few feet over the marble tiles, losing my grip on the sword. I lay there not wanting to move, trying to figure out if the fall had broken anything major. My hands ached from holding onto the hilt so tight.

Grogochs crowded around me. They leapt and cheered and pulled me to my feet. Some patted me on the back and one gave me a shy hug. Another puckered his lips and jumped up and down as though he wanted to kiss me.

William lumbered over to me, displaying a toothy grin. "They like you. They admire courage." He bowed his head. "As do I, milady. I am in your debt and since you didn't burst into flames, the sword called *Sea*

Pirate belongs to you."

I kept the kissing Grogoch at arm's length. "Wait. Burst into flames?"

William's eyes widened, trying to look innocent. "Didn't I tell you? I'm sure I said something about a curse and if you're not worthy, the blade would set you on fire. Oh, well. All's well that ends well. I blame the pain. There is always a small risk in removing an enchanted sword. That's the first thing a champion learns."

I narrowed my gaze. "You should have told me."

"Did I mention that when you swing the sword in an arc, it creates a rainbow?"

I ignored the reference to champions and the part about rainbows. I was learning that in this magical realm, anything living was tossed into a group. If you weren't one of the gods or goddesses, or a plant or animal, then you were either a member of the Sidhe, a goblin, or a champion. Humans were lumped into the plant or animal category. I guessed I should be pleased he'd suggested I was a champion. Except champions usually went on lost cause quests and died. Swell.

I crossed my arms over my chest. "If we are going to be friends, we can't keep secrets. Especially ones that are harmful. Explain yourself."

"Friends?" he said with a hopeful expression.

I narrowed my eyes and glared.

"Very well. If someone is unworthy, with evil intentions for using the blade, the moment they touch the hilt, it ignites into a fire so hot it burns the person…"

I held up my hand. "I get the point."

He nudged the sword over to me with his paw.

"No, you misunderstand. You didn't burst into flames. That should make you happy. Did I mention the sword has the power to create a rainbow in the air?"

I nodded, knowing he was trying to make amends. I swung the blade in an arc over my head. Nothing.

"Try again. It has to get to know you."

I did as he asked. I lunged a few times and swung the blade back and forth in front of me. I thought the weapon would be heavy, but the balance and weight were perfect for my size, as though a sword master had made it for me personally. I was also surprised at how easy it was to wield. But still no rainbows. A little discouraged, I said, "I must be doing it wrong. Are there any rules I should know about?"

His grin turned into a self-satisfied smile, which seemed odd on a dragon. "Can't tell you anything more. Part of the conditions of my enchantment. Long list of dos and don'ts. Very wordy. Sometimes I think sorceresses are frustrated bards. They should be writing poetry, not spells."

"Okay," I said, realizing my new dragon friend had issues with sorceresses. I probably would as well if I were cursed.

When I started to press him on what he *could* tell me, like maybe why he was cursed in the first place or why the sword was named *Sea Pirate*, smoke began to bellow from the castle's entrance.

An old man wearing druid-style robes rushed through the cloud of smoke, beating sparks out of his sleeves and long beard. "I do not know what happened," he said, doubling over to catch his breath. "I was mixing a new potion for William and something went terribly, terribly wrong. All my vials are exploding like fireworks."

He ducked as a fireball shot out of the entrance and splashed into the moat, spraying everyone with a wave of muck and mud. A few Grogochs popped into sight to see why their home was sizzling, took one look at the smoke, and disappeared again. The old man slumped to the ground.

"Mug Ruith," Biróg screamed, rushing to his side.

The air crackled like the aftermath of a lightning storm. I tried to rub off the moat mud. It clung to my fingers like spider webs mixed with stinky garbage. A Grogoch popped in beside me and handed me a bundle of grass. He pantomimed how to use it to clean my clothes. I nodded my thanks as two more Grogochs popped into view.

William scrunched up his sizeable nose. "The goo is one of the Grogochs' weapons and discourages strangers from invading their home. It also helps with the castle's defense. If not removed, the liquid from the moat reeks worse than seaweed baking in the hot sun and clings to the skin and clothes for days. We might not see an enemy coming, but there's no denying the smell."

With Biróg's help, Mug Ruith stood. "No time for explanations. Our home is about to explode. Biróg, Lugh, I'll need your help as well. Mac Tíre, protect our guests. William, lead the way."

William nodded his massive head. "On it." He winked at me. "Stay here. I'll be right back." He paused. "Just in case. It was very nice meeting you, Grace."

Chapter Twelve

While I was trying to figure out how the dragon had known my name, I noticed that Síofra stood near the castle's entrance with a lost expression, as though caught between worlds. I knew how she felt. She wanted to help as much as I did, but we'd been classified as "guests."

"Well done," Mac Tíre said, motioning to my sword. He looked at me for so long I noticed his eyes weren't so much brown as amber, with green flecks of gold. He blinked, and they turned a darker shade as he glanced toward Síofra. "You were right about Grace. *Sea Pirate* suits her. You, though, will have to stay out of the way a little longer."

I wanted to defend Síofra as I had all our lives, insist she could do anything she wanted to do, despite the condition of her arm.

"Síofra can help."

"Grace, you don't even know what's coming," Mac Tíre said.

"Síofra can help," I repeated, holding my ground. In many ways, Síofra and I were alike. People kept underestimating us.

Flower fairies erupted from the trees in a splash of color, panic, and confusion. The few remaining Grogochs popped out of sight. The fairies veered north, then south, and then straight toward the darkening sky as though there were no safe places to hide. Branches shuddered, dropping their leaves.

"The Dullahan are coming," Mac Tíre announced. "Hard to tell how many."

It felt as though bony fingers grabbed my throat and squeezed. I couldn't breathe. I'd heard stories about the Dullahan in the same way most children had heard such tales of horror. Stories with cautionary tales and cloaked meanings that were told late at night when the moon was full.

If a parent warned it was dangerous to go outside late at night, the child might think the mother or father overprotective. If, on the other hand, the parent claimed they'd risk being stolen by a mud-covered Bullybods who hid in swamps or bogs, the child would be in bed under the covers, feigning sleep. And yes, I spoke from experience.

Like many stories, the Headless Horsemen held a pinch of truth. The Dullahan, or dark men, were the embodiment of death and were the mercenaries of Crom Dubh. This Death Lord demanded human sacrifice and his favored form of murdering his victims was decapitation.

I shivered as Síofra came up beside me, her face as pale as the moon. "I thought we'd have more time," she said.

Mac Tíre tensed, shielding us with one arm as he drew his sword with the other.

A headless rider burst from the woods. He paused at the edge of the drawbridge. His horse was three times the size of any I'd ever seen. His eyes glowed as though they were on fire and smoke curled from his flared nostrils. The horse reared; hooves blazed with fire as they churned the air. This Dullahan seemed to be waiting for a signal, or maybe for us to die of fright. The latter seemed more likely.

Fear clutched at my chest, forcing the breath from my lungs. The rider held his head outstretched in his hand as though it were a prize he wanted to share. He lifted it by hair that was long, black, and looked like it hadn't been washed in a hundred years. The eyes darted in their sockets in a frantic dance, like fireflies caught in a jar. Worms crawled from his nose and snakes from his mouth.

I moved back a step, fighting the impulse to run. "How do we kill it?" My hands trembled as I raised my sword.

"You can't," Mac Tíre said. "He's already dead. And once he begins his hunt for a soul, he's unstoppable."

"What about Biróg and Mug Ruith? One is a goddess and the other a druid."

"Their magic is powerless against Headless Horsemen," Síofra said. She removed a gold brooch from her cape and handed it to Mac Tíre. "But they fear gold. It may keep you alive." Her voice quivered like a harp cord strung too tight. "I wish I could do more. If only…"

"I cannot accept your gift," he said. "It belonged to your mother." He looped his finger around a chain hidden under his shirt. "Besides, I have gold. And as for you, do not worry, your time will come." Then he turned toward me and spoke in his older-brother voice. A tone I found annoying for some reason. "If this works, promise me you'll go with Mug Ruith and the dragon. Find out why the gods and goddesses are being secretive. That's not like them. Lugh also knows more than he's letting on. If I don't come back, you need to finish what we started."

The weight of what he said settled in. He didn't think he'd survive. He was sacrificing himself so we could escape. "You're not facing this thing alone. I'm wearing my mother's gold ring and Síofra has a gold brooch. If Síofra's right, we have a better chance if we stay together. Besides, I have a weapon. The Sword of *Foghlaí Muir*." I wasn't sure why I thought that would make a difference, but one look at Mac Tíre's expression and I knew I had been right to bring it up.

He gave me an unreadable look.

"You're not facing this alone," I repeated.

He grinned. "I'm the only one who can. The plan is to steal his head. Dullahans are afraid of wolves."

"But how does that help?"

The Dullahan thundered over the drawbridge straight toward us. "Hold your ground and wait for my orders," Mac Tíre advised. "The Dullahan are used to people running from them."

My throat constricted. Of course people ran, Headless Horsemen were crazy-scary.

Mac Tíre was right. The Dullahan seemed confused that he didn't have to chase us. Sparks flew as his horse pawed the ground then reared. Hooves tore the air. The Dullahan's disembodied head let out a scream. The sound traveled toward us, grating across my skin.

Mac Tíre shouted. "When I count to three, run to his left. I'll go right."

Knowing Mac Tíre had a plan was calming. I was on fear-overload, but this way I didn't have to think. All

I had to do was follow orders.

The Dullahan moved so fast he was a blur of black and silver. Startled, I bit down so hard on my lip I drew blood. Mac Tíre counted down. Three. Two. One.

We raced to our positions.

Our enemy looked confused, unsure who to attack first. That was the first part of Mac Tíre's plan. Assessing that Síofra and I were the weakest link was the second. The Dullahan turned first his head, then his body toward us. I admit the maneuver was a little creepy. My stomach roiled.

The Dullahan's blade was longer than I was tall and glowed like an angry, tinder-dry forest fire. He drew his sword over his head and attacked. He knocked Síofra out of the way with the flat of his sword. She hit her head on the ground. I moved toward her, but he blocked my path and lunged.

I ducked. Air swooshed as the blade passed over my head. He roared, as surprised as I was that he'd missed. He swung again. I rose and blocked his attack.

The contact vibrated through me. I expected my blade would be sliced in two as if it were made of butter instead of forged steel. It didn't. *Sea Pirate* held strong. My blade shimmered in a burst of color and power. Its rainbow lights drew a blood-chilling scream from the Dullahan that sent shivers through every nerve in my body.

My father said a warrior's goal was to feel one with his blade. I'd never known what he'd meant until now. The sword was part of me, making me stronger, braver.

The Dullahan hesitated, as though reassessing his enemy. The snakes that were coiled in his mouth hissed. His eyes burned a deeper blood-red. He arced his weapon over his head, but his hesitation was his undoing.

His choice of attacking me first had given Mac Tíre the time he needed to circle around and surprise our enemy from behind. With the Dullahan's full attention on me, Mac Tíre vaulted onto the back of his horse.

The Dullahan roared in protest. His demon horse reared, trying to unseat Mac Tíre. The tactic failed.

With Mac Tíre still holding on, the Dullahan reined his stallion back onto the bridge and sped into the woods.

Night swallowed day the same moment Mac Tíre disappeared, as though the two were linked. Dazed, Síofra pushed to her feet, rubbing her head. She stared in the direction we'd last seen Mac Tíre and the Dullahan. Mac Tíre had saved us, but at what cost?

This was worse than when I had been below ground with the Mouldywarp.

Mac Tíre had said someone sent the Dullahan, and that Lugh and the gods and goddesses knew more than they were saying. I felt helpless. We had to find Mac Tíre, but how could we chase after a creature that moved faster than a shooting star?

****

William bounded from the castle entrance, belched out smoke and soot, and then promptly turned the color of molten silver. He craned his long neck, examining his body. "Silver. Now that's more like it."

Síofra and I rushed over to him, launching into a detailed account of the Headless Horseman, his attack, and how Mac Tíre had risked his life to save us. William seemed oblivious. He ignored us and craned his neck, admiring his scales. I thought Síofra was going to smack him. I would have helped.

Biróg and Mug Ruith's entrance was even more disappointing. They didn't even acknowledge us. Biróg launched into a heated discussion with Mug Ruith on why replacing building materials was Michelangelo's fault. According to Biróg, Michelangelo insisted only pure-white Carrara marble from Italy was appropriate for his statues of David and the Pieta. Because of the artist's reputation and success, every sculptor wanted Carrara marble, which drove up the price.

But when he mentioned there was nothing wrong with his calculations that could have caused an explosion, Biróg stopped her marble tirade in mid-sentence.

"I disagree. You almost blew up the castle."

Mug Ruith began weaving his floor-length beard into braids. "The potions weren't supposed to explode. Fizz perhaps, foam most certainly, but not explode." His voice was low, distracted.

William rubbed his stomach. "There's nothing fizzy about how my stomach feels. I have indigestion. Do you think I'm dying? My tongue feels funny. I think I'm pale. Am I pale?"

I couldn't stand it any longer. "Enough!" I shouted. William, Biróg, and Mug Ruith all turned toward me at the same time. I clenched my fists at my sides. "While you were trying to save your precious marble, we were attacked by a Headless Horseman and Mac Tíre was captured."

Mug Ruith smoothed his hand over his beard. "Are you sure? No one survives a Dullahan attack," he said in a condescending tone. "Where is Mac Tíre? He'll be able to sort out this misunderstanding."

"I just told you. He saved Síofra and me, by jumping on the back of the Dullahan's horse. With or without your help, Síofra and I are going to rescue him."

Síofra stood beside me for support, her expression fierce. "By the way, where is Lugh?"

"He is not with you?" Biróg said.

Biróg and Mug Ruith exchanged glances with William, but their expressions looked as readable as tree bark.

Mug Ruith said. "I'd wager my druid's wand that the Femorians are behind the attack."

"And captured my poor Lugh," Biróg said, wringing her hands.

Mug Ruith patted her on the arm. "There, there. We don't know that for sure."

"You are probably correct," Biróg said with a nod, taking in a slow breath. "Lugh is a smart lad. He may have decided to join the Red Branch warriors on Beg Ara after all until the Book is recovered. I'm more convinced than ever that Femorians are behind the theft. They've been bitter ever since their banishment, waiting for an opportunity to seek their revenge. They lived in Ireland before the Tuatha's arrival. Some say the Femorians were descended from Noah's son, Ham, and his followers were survivors of one of Earth's great floods."

"More likely they were seafarers from Africa," Mug Ruith argued. "Ireland was caught up in endless war. When the Tuatha arrived from their sky-ships in a cloud of mist, promising peace, we were filled with hope. To prove their intentions were pure, they burned their vessels, showing they planned to stay."

"Their reasons were more complicated," Biróg added. "They destroyed their ships to avoid detection from whoever had driven them from their home. At first, the Tuatha and Femorians coexisted in peace, intermarried, and prospered."

William rolled his eyes; evidently, he'd heard this history lesson before. He ambled off to take a nap. Síofra and I tried to make our escape, but Mug Ruith pulled us back with a stern look.

"If you are to understand our enemies, you must know how it all started. Peace in Ireland was followed by tragedy. The Tuatha's king, Nuada, lost his arm in battle, and under their traditions, a king or queen cannot rule unless they are physically whole."

I glanced over at Síofra and felt a wave of protectiveness. I knew she wanted to be a fairy queen. "That's a stupid rule."

Síofra gave me a weak smile of gratitude as she rubbed her withered arm. "Wasn't Nuada fitted with a silver arm to make him whole again?"

Mug Ruith nodded. "Yes, but Bres was a cruel ruler, and refused to return the kingship when Nuada recovered. At first, Bres only enacted unfair taxes. When that failed to crush the Tuathan spirit, he enslaved them." Mug Ruith held a shaking hand over his mouth, unable to continue.

I cleared my throat. "Thank you for the history lesson, but Síofra and I are leaving. Our friend Mac Tíre is missing and we promised when we started this journey that we'd look out for each other." Síofra and I hadn't discussed it, but her slight nod confirmed she agreed. We started to back away, but Mug Ruith held out his staff in front of us.

"I forbid it." He raised his staff and struck it on the marble steps.

My ears rang with a deafening sound. White smoke curled around me like a shroud, shutting out the light.

Chapter Thirteen

The next thing I knew, I was hiking up a mountain. In the rain and in the dark. It was close to midnight: the moon and stars were in hiding and the only light came from the druid's staff. I tugged on Mug Ruith's sleeve. "Why am I here? I have to get back. Síofra and I need to rescue Mac Tíre."

He raised his staff. A white light blinded me and for a moment my vision was fuzzy. "If you are rested, we will continue."

I rubbed my eyes, trying to remember if he'd answered my question. I was worried about my friends. I was pretty sure he'd said they were safe. Hadn't he? He vanished around a corner for a moment. Feeling anxious I'd get lost, I hurried to catch up, but that was an odd thought since I never got lost. When I was close enough to speak to him, I changed my mind. I was sure my friends were safe. Otherwise, why would I be here?

The only break in the silence was a rhythmic knocking or ticking-type noise. It grew louder the higher we climbed and sounded like a family of woodpeckers building a fortress on top of the mountain.

Water cascaded over rocks on my right, and on my left was the valley of Tir na nÓg. A wall of mountain Rowan trees, dense with white flowers and red berries, formed an effective barrier. Every once in a while, I could see William flying overhead. After the exploding-potion incident, I was glad he was around. I'd overheard him and Mug Ruith discussing that they expected another attack.

"Did William tell you about the legend surrounding your sword?" Mug Ruith said over his shoulder.

I rested my hand on the hilt of *Sea Pirate* protectively. I didn't want the druid to tell me it was cursed and that I had to throw it back into some slimy bog. *Sea Pirate* was the first weapon I'd felt belonged to me, not a heavy, ill-suited weapon I'd borrowed for sword practice and had to return, or one made of wood the sword master had given me without my father's knowledge.

"It's an interesting story," Mug Ruith said. "The sword was thrown away by accident and I'm not sure if she wants it back, but I'll ask. Oh, here we are."

Mug Ruith's response didn't make me feel secure that I could keep the sword. Who was this mysterious "she" he'd mentioned?

I gripped the hilt of the sword tighter. I liked having a weapon of my own that wasn't made of wood, and I wanted to keep it.

The druid drew a branch aside with his staff, exposing a level area devoid of trees. It stretched out before me. Pathways wove over the surface in what seemed to be random shades of yellow, red, and orange as though someone had thrown of a basket of ribbons over the ground.

William landed a short distance away and folded his wings. He nodded toward me as though confirming that he was here to protect me.

Mug Ruith struck his staff on the edge of a bright red pathway. The glass and wooden beads he'd woven into his beard jangled with the sudden movement like wind chimes caught in a breeze. He nodded toward the dragon and raised his voice.

"William, stand guard. When they discover they failed to blow up the castle, they'll try to locate my workshop."

The druid mentioned a workshop, but all I saw was a strand of trees on the far edge of the plateau, which must be where the ticking sound was coming from. No doubt a whole family of woodpeckers busy pecking out their homes.

My mother taught me to honor and respect the elderly and never tease those whose memories were "time-weathered," as she liked to say. So I chewed on a corner of my lower lip rather than point out that not only was the mountain remote, cold, and lonely, but there wasn't so much as a small cottage, let alone a druid's workshop in sight.

Perhaps a workshop had been here when the Tuatha de Danaan ruled Ireland, before the wars, betrayal, and destruction. The remnants of a system of pathways suggested that possibility. But all other traces were gone. Maybe Mug Ruith was like those who remembered events that had happened decades in the past clearer than those that had occurred after their morning meal.

Then Mug Ruith did something odd, even for him. He counted out three long, measured strides on a red path, turned left for six more strides on a yellow path, and made a sharp left turn onto an orange path and walked an additional nine.

He stopped abruptly, drew out a set of keys from the folds of his robe, selected one painted red, and jabbed it in the air. Nothing happened. He frowned and repeated the action.

Click.

He gave a nod, shot me a satisfied grin, and turned the key a full circle.

Double doors, the color of molten copper, materialized and swung inward. Walls appeared and rippled like panels of silk caught in a breeze. Light sliced through the air, blinding me. I rubbed my eyes and tried to focus. The walls disappeared again. The only thing visible was an open door standing in the middle of the meadow.

****

Still grinning, Mug Ruith winked. "What do you think of my workshop?" He spread his arms and looked as excited as a child with a new toy. "Biróg is obsessed with marble. Too dense for my purposes. I prefer mirrors. It was my great friend Leonardo da Vinci's idea. He was a famous inventor and painter, you know. Mirrors reflect the clouds and surrounding forest and turn my workshop almost invisible to the naked eye. The illusion fooled me a time or two. The pathways were my idea and hold the clue to the location of the entrance. Otherwise, I'd spend most of my time trying to find the keyhole."

Mug Ruith had reason to be proud. Unless you bumped into it by accident, his workshop was invisible. My father could use this type of illusion either to sneak past an enemy ship unnoticed or surprise a merchant vessel loaded down with exotic spices, silks, and precious metals. Thinking of my father made me sad. I was no closer to finding out what had happened to him. I needed answers. But the farther into the quest I ventured, the more questions arose.

As I followed Mug Ruith through a series of hallways, the noises I'd heard earlier grew louder. They were vaguely familiar. They were uniform and measured as though each one was timed precisely. When the druid shoved open a door the source was obvious. Not woodpeckers. Not even close.

Instead of birds, clocks were grouped together like families at an Irish celebration. The clocks we had in our castle were captured from a French merchant ship, but none were as wondrous as Mug Ruith's.

Proud grandfather clocks stood watch along the perimeter. There were clocks as large as William and ones smaller than my cat. One perched on top of a statue of a ceramic elephant and another served as the face of a knight in shining armor. Clocks in every imaginable shape and size hung on walls, rolled on wheels, were suspended from the ceiling, or clustered on tables.

I'd heard stories about druids, and none of them were flattering. Legends stressed their wickedness. According to the stories, they dealt in black magic, conjured spells, and demanded animal sacrifices.

Mug Ruith didn't fit the description except the spell and magic potion part. He was more like an eccentric uncle or kindly grandfather.

I reached toward a clock shaped in the image of a life-size raven. It tilted its mechanical head inquisitively as though aware of my presence. Small, circular wheels resembling eyes rolled on its clock face. Its beak creaked, opened, and snapped at my fingers. I back away. Message received. *Don't touch.*

Mug Ruith chuckled. "Robert the Raven is a

favorite of mine. Quite life-like, and like his flesh and blood counterpart, he's a fickle creature. Robert is your friend one moment and untrustworthy the next. He also never tells the correct time. Always a few minutes late. But I find that flaws are always more interesting." He glanced over his workroom with a pleased expression. "Clocks are a hobby of mine. I find it helps me think when I have a puzzle to solve."

A gong struck, and in less time than it took to draw a breath, all the clocks in the room struck midnight. Some chimed. The ones resembling animals and birds chirped, squawked, or roared. Not to be outdone, the grandfather clocks chimed in rich baritone or played melodies.

Mug Ruith seemed oblivious to the clatter. Me? Not so much. I covered my ears to muffle the sound. I preferred the murmured whispers of the sea.

"Ah," he said. "They are reminding me to give you your gift. Every champion needs one. Follow me."

"Champion?" My thoughts froze on the word. William also had called me a champion. But Mug Ruith hadn't noticed my questioning response. He was already halfway across the chamber.

I hurried after him. For a man as old as many of the oak trees in our forest, he moved so fast I could barely keep pace.

With the sound of the clocks fading, I followed him down a wide corridor. The open-air ceiling framed a pewter-gray sky. Patches of clouds shaped like ships and prancing horses floated overhead in the glow of the moon and scattered stars.

Mug Ruith led me into another workroom. Instead of clocks, this one housed inventions.

Some I recognized as weapons. There were numerous cannons and catapults designed to launch boulders big enough to breach castle walls. Other machines and their purpose were as big a mystery to me as Mug Ruith was. There was a round coach-like vehicle with long, horizontal blades attached to the roof and a suit of armor sprouting hollow tubes out the top of its helmet.

"Leonardo da Vinci," Mug Ruith said with a quick nod of his head toward the mysterious inventions, as though that were all the explanation needed. "The one with the blades flies in the sky. The suit of armor with tubes allows a man to breathe under water." His lips pinched together as though he'd tasted sour milk. "I have only a few of his inventions. The Vatican seized the lion's share. Leonardo was a true genius. Although he denied any relationship to the Tuatha, we knew differently." Mug Ruith's voice trailed off as though he were engulfed in a wave of memories and pain.

It was then I noticed a shadow move across the sky.

William circled above us, landing on the rim of the roof. He seemed distracted, nervous, as though expecting trouble.

"What's wrong with William?" I said.

"He does not like being silver," he said absently, although traces of the melancholy in his voice still lingered around the edges. "When we are done here, I will try out a new potion. Orange, perhaps. Or blue. Biróg likes blue."

"I don't think that's the reason."

"Come. You must see my collection of weapons."

That got my attention.

William lifted off from the roof and disappeared behind a bank of clouds as the druid thumbed his chin. "Odd, the harp is missing." He shrugged away his concern and opened the lid of a carved box.

The lining was a deep forest-green with seed pearls sewn into the fabric at even intervals, creating a pillow effect. Cushioned in the center lay an inch-wide curved necklace called a torque, crafted of solid gold. Warriors had worn torques like this one into battle around the time of the first kings of Ireland.

Mug Ruith held it reverently as though it might break. "This was Leonardo's last invention. He knew he would not always be around, so he discovered a way to imprint his knowledge into the invisible symbols etched into the gold. Whoever wears this torque is gifted with the ability to operate any of his machines. Quite extraordinary, actually. He was inspired by the legend of Fionntán the Wise. Fionntán survived the great flood that engulfed the world by changing himself into a salmon. He lived for thousands of years, gathering the knowledge of the world so that he could advise the kings and queens of Ireland. A heady responsibility."

Mug Ruith peered at me over the rim of his spectacles with that expression adults have when they think they've said something clever. Except I'd heard the story of the Salmon of Knowledge before and I'd never liked the ending.

"Didn't Finn MacCool eat the salmon to gain its knowledge? If I were the smartest person in the world, I'd turn myself into something scarier than a fish. Or at least something not edible."

"I prefer his more formal name, Fionn mac Cumhaill." Mug Ruith set the torque back down.

"Perhaps it is too soon for the torque."

I reached for his arm. "Was that the warrior who defeated Lord Aillén with a magic spear?"

Mug Ruith gave an impatient flick of his hand in the direction of a spear mounted to the wall. "Classic story. Warrior kills bad guy. Frees land. Wins hand of princess. The usual." Mug Ruith lifted a box from a shelf and dusted the top with his sleeve. "This is more like it. Arm bracelets. They will help you gain safe passage as well as entrance to the training fields on the Isle of Skye's Shadow Island. Ireland's best-known champion, Cuchulainn, and members of the Red Branch, trained with the warrior queen, Aoife, and her sisters. I've arranged with William to give you a ride. You leave immediately."

Something in the back of my mind held me back. An elusive memory. People I cared about were in danger. The memory snapped out of focus. A voice in my head argued that training to become a warrior was what I'd always wanted.

The room darkened as an object moved overhead, blocking out the light. At first, I thought William had returned, but he wasn't anywhere in sight. What looked like a ship hovered above the workshop.

Mug Ruith and Biróg mentioned that the Tuatha had arrived in sky-ships, but I admit, I had been only half listening, believing it was more legend than reality. I shook my head in disbelief. A wide-bodied galley rode the wind as smooth as most ships sail the high seas. I couldn't look away. I shouldn't have been surprised. In the last few days, I'd met fairies, dragons, and monsters I'd thought were legends and myths. Why not a ship that flew?

It was a beauty. Its sails puffed out proudly as though it knew how grand it looked as it moved closer. My opinion changed. The building materials were all wrong. "Is the ship made out of…"

"Bones," Mug Ruith finished. "Goblin bones, to be precise."

From this distance, the crew looked like ants swarming over a picnic table. Some climbed the riggings and unfurled another sail for added speed. Others scurried to the cannons and lit the fuses.

Smoke curled out of the barrels of the cannons.

A boom cracked the calm.

We were under attack.

Chapter Fourteen

Breathing fire, William flew straight toward the warship.

Cannons could blow a ship apart, leaving behind a skeletal shell of burned-out wood and charred remains. I shuddered to think what they would do to a flesh and blood dragon.

"We have to help William," I said with rising panic.

Mug Ruith put his hand on my shoulder, which did nothing to calm my nerves. "Nothing to worry about. Usually, pirates fire off a few warning shots and submit their demands. What they really want is gold, not confrontation. A price is negotiated, and they leave. William will ensure their demands aren't unreasonable. This dance has gone on for centuries."

I wasn't convinced it was only bluster. The cannons were aimed at William. Father had said if your goal was to scare a captain into submission, you didn't sink his ship and kill his crew. With everyone dead and the ship at the bottom of the sea, negotiations were a moot point and any valuable cargo lost.

Smoke billowed out of the cannons, then another crack. I yelled for William to get out of the way. As though he'd heard me, he tilted his wings and rolled in the air, out of range and behind a cloud.

William outmaneuvered the cannons once, but

unfortunately, the gunners were already making readjustments. The odds weren't in the dragon's favor.

"They'll kill William."

Mug Ruith looked visibly shaken. "I do not understand. True, their raids were becoming more frequent of late. We thought it was because of a higher turnover. Crews and captains consist of runaways from every corner of the magical and mortal realm. They fight amongst themselves and are hard to control. More of a nuisance than a real threat. Something has changed."

The crew raised a flag. At first, I thought it might be a white flag of truce, which meant they wanted to surrender or negotiate. But it wasn't white. It was black, and the image wasn't clear from this angle.

Mug Ruith's staff clattered to the floor as he started opening drawers and cupboards, searching for something. He scattered boxes and garment pouches over the room. He checked one bank of shelves before moving to another.

I was about to ask if I could help when he gave a loud cheer and snatched a long rod-like object off a top shelf. Books and rolls of parchment tumbled around him unnoticed.

He held a telescope—that much I could tell. Only it was four times the size of the ones my father owned. Mug Ruith mounted it on a tripod and aimed it at the sky. He looked into the glass eyepiece and stood there so long I heard the ticking of the clocks in the next room. When he stepped back, his face was the color of ash.

He shook his head, repeating the same word over and over. "Impossible." He moved farther and farther away as though distance could alter his discovery.

I approached slowly, concerned that if I moved too quickly he'd dissolve into a panic-puddle. Whatever he'd seen had him as paralyzed with fear, as my limbs had been when the Mouldywarp had covered me with green drool.

He pointed at the telescope and muttered incoherently. I took his place at the telescope and at first the image was blurred and reminded me of the mushroom veil. Instead of looking into a forest, I saw clouds and patches of gray sky. I adjusted the focus but couldn't see either the ship or William.

They'd both disappeared.

I adjusted the focus and moved the telescope from left to right and back again. It didn't help that the sky was darkening as though it too were against me. Just when I thought I'd never find them, a puff of metal-gray smoke snapped into view in a southwesterly direction, followed by muffled popping sounds.

"Cannon fire," I breathed out slowly, hoping not to startle Mug Ruith. When my comment was met with silence, I refocused in the direction of the sound. As expected, the ship was farther away which meant so was William. I adjusted the focus. The telescope was so powerful I could make out facial features.

The crew scrambled to reload. The captain stood at the helm, bathed in shadows. I couldn't get a clear view. His body language told me he wasn't having his best day. He shook his fist, shouting to someone who had his back turned away from me.

"William succeeded in drawing the enemy away from Tir na nÓg," I said to Mug Ruith. "The pirate ship's no longer a threat."

I glanced over my shoulder, prepared to see a relieved druid. Not so much. Mug Ruith stood in the exact same place as before, his head angled toward the sky. His skin had a death-like appearance, as though all the blood had drained from his body.

"The flag is all wrong," he said as he whirled around and fled the room.

I turned back to the ship, trying to figure out what had frightened him. Most pirate ships' flags were black with a white image of a skull-and-crossbones. You knew you would receive neither mercy nor justice, only death. At first glance, the image on the flag of the sky-ship looked ordinary. A large circle that contained intertwining Celtic swirls. The images moved inside the circle as though alive, changing shape, reforming. Then I saw the image that had frightened Mug Ruith.

A fire breathing, two-headed dragon.

Just then, the person the captain was arguing with turned in my direction. He glanced toward me as though he knew I was spying on him and didn't care.

His lips curled in a smile.

I stumbled back. "Oh, no."

****

"John Dee." My voice cracked when I said his name aloud.

There had to be an explanation. I wanted to believe he was being held prisoner. That I'd misread his expression. After all, the ship was a long way away. I looked through the telescope again to double-check.

The ship was gone.

But I knew it had been John Dee. My dilemma was, whom to tell? Mug Ruith and the Tuatha knew he'd stolen the Book. They'd thought he would turn it over either to the Femorians or smuggle it into England. Maybe he had a good reason and was trying to keep it safe. If I could talk to him, convince him to give it back.

But first I had to get Fionn mac Cumhaill's spear. I grabbed it, but for some reason the bracelets caught my attention. I tucked both spear and the bracelets under my cloak and hurried into the clock room only to be chased out by their accusatory ticking. John Dee had betrayed us, and I was still making excuses for him.

He was a thief.

But so was I.

I hurried through the corridors and pushed opened the door to the outside. It was still raining. No longer soft and gentle, it poured out of the sky with vengeance. William had just landed. He looked like someone had attacked him with a battering ram. His silver scales were bent and covered with scorch marks. He moved with a limp and held his right wing out at an odd angle.

William had risked so much. Had I the right to keep the knowledge that I'd seen John Dee a secret? When the dragon nodded a greeting, I ran over and wrapped my arms around his neck. His dragon scales were surprisingly warm. Shaking, I held on tighter, not sure whom I could trust with what I'd seen. If John Dee had been kidnapped, I owed him a chance to explain. I had to find out the truth. I had to get on that ship.

William winced. "Ow. You are crushing my throat." His breathing was labored, and there was a rattling sound when he inhaled that sounded like rocks rolling around in a metal bucket.

I pulled away. "Sorry. Where does it hurt?"

"Everywhere."

The expression in his eyes brought tears to my own. He was in pain and trying to make a joke. "You'll need a healer. Biróg?" I offered. I didn't want to suggest Mug Ruith. He was useless at the moment. I worried that whatever he was afraid of might affect his judgment and instead of mixing a healing potion, by mistake he might concoct a poisonous brew.

"Not necessary." William kept still as though even slight movement hurt. "Dragons heal on their own, as long as the injuries are minor. Mine aren't as bad as they look."

"Well, that's good to hear, since they look as though someone used you as a practice dummy. You were very brave."

He grinned and winced all at the same time. "Managed to torch their main sail. They'll have to dock their ship for repairs."

"All the more reason to stay here until we learn the truth." Mug Ruith's voice slid into the space between us like a knife cutting through air. A book was tucked in the crook of his arm. The leather straps and wax seals that bound it together were ripped apart. Mug Ruith looked like he had aged twenty years or more since I'd seen him moments ago. Which made him look about one hundred and fifty.

William's gaze drifted toward the book. "You said it was stolen."

"This is only a copy of the Book of Invasions. It is all here, down to the last battle. There is also a copy in each of the four cities of Tir na nÓg, along with one of the four symbols of the Tuathan power. But the copies lack the magic and power of the original. The original was on loan to Oghy U and we were assured it would be safe." Mug Ruith sighed. "Sadly, there was a traitor in our midst. The Tuatha should never have allowed the Femorians to remain in Ireland. It is the end of our world, both human as well as magical."

Chapter Fifteen

William huffed out a puff of smoke. "Must you always be so dramatic? If this druid gig doesn't work out, you could make a living on stage. One of the flower fairies said William Shakespeare will be born in England in about twenty years and will be the greatest bard of all time. Maybe he'll give you a job as an actor in one of his plays."

"Actor? Careful, William. I'll have you know that I am a fifth-generation druid. You cannot wake up one morning and decide that you are going to be the Tuathan high priest. It takes years to gain the power and skill and confidence, not to mention trust. You, my scaly friend, are a fine one to criticize. Tell Grace the real reason a sorceress turned you into a dragon."

Steam bellowed out of William's flared nostrils. "Careful druid. We have an agreement."

Mug Ruith and William were older than me and yet were the ones exhibiting childish temper tantrums instead of trying to come up with a plan.

"Stop it, both of you. Could someone please tell me why the world is ending? According to Biróg, the Book's disappearance caused changes in the past, which impact the present and affected weather patterns in the four cities of Tir na nÓg. If it's not stopped, the human's realm will also experience changes. Biróg's theory is that if we return the Book, time will heal itself. Problem solved. What am I missing?"

"Problem solved? Problem solved?" Mug Ruith's voice rose, like the crest of a wave, smashing against the shore. "It is not that simple and it's only a theory. Nothing like this has ever happened. The world is…"

"Coming to an end," William said, finishing the druid's sentence. We heard, and as much as it pains me to say, you're right. If the Goblin race succeeds, they will create a world where the portals of the Land of the Dead will remain open and evil will rule unchecked."

"A never-ending Halloween," Mug Ruith added. "The symbol of a two-headed dragon is troubling. It means they have more allies than we first thought. I suspect the Milesians are working with them as well. We should stay here until we learn what they really want."

"Milesians? Aren't they the same people who defeated the Tuatha in the last battle?" I asked.

Mug Ruith nodded. "I hope I am wrong. If not, we have a bigger problem. They have the ability to create floods."

"As in the floods that cover fields," I asked hopefully.

William lowered his head. "As in the floods that submerge islands."

I started to pace, hoping that would help me think. The druids built clocks; I paced. "William, you said they'd have to anchor and repair their damaged sky-ship."

William narrowed his gaze. "What are you suggesting?"

"I plan to stow away onboard their ship. They may know the location of the Book." I wasn't ready to share that I'd seen John Dee.

"You plan to stow away on a Femorian ship?" William repeated. "Question: where would you like your remains buried, providing the Femorians turn over your body?"

"Not funny."

"It wasn't meant to be."

****

William's message was clear. If I boarded the Femorian ship, I would die. My resolve wavered. Why was I feeling so unsure?

"Release Grace from your spell." Mac Tíre galloped toward us, his sword drawn. He reined his horse a few feet from me. Síofra slid from behind him and rushed over, enfolding me in a crushing hug.

The moment we made contact, my memories surrounding Mac Tíre and Síofra flooded back. Our being attacked by the Dullahan, Mac Tíre risking his life to save us, Síofra and I wanting to rescue him.

"You must leave!" Mug Ruith shouted, his voice sounding desperate. "Grace is safe here. You have my promise."

"I don't trust your promises," Mac Tíre said. "Grace is coming with us."

Mug Ruith raised his staff. "Stand back," he ordered. "Grace must stay with me until this is over and the danger past. I'm warning you. I'll turn you and Síofra into…into frogs."

"No, you will not," Síofra said. "You cannot. We are protected."

Mac Tíre moved closer. "Be a good druid, take your dragon back to the marble castle and untie Biróg."

"You tied up a goddess?" I said.

Mac Tíre shrugged.

"If you harmed Biróg…" Mug Ruith threatened.

"Relax. Biróg owed me a favor. I just reminded her. I only tied her up to keep her from trying to escape and warn you before I could reach Grace. I should warn you: Biróg is more upset with you than me. Something about misrepresenting the real problem."

Angry, Mug Ruith slammed his staff on the ground. In a flash of light, both he and William vanished.

****

With Mug Ruith and William gone, Síofra explained that the druid had blocked my recent memories. It was a common trick the Sidhe used to keep humans in the Otherworld. I no longer thought of Mug Ruith as the kindly grandfather type. Nor did I feel guilty for snatching the spear and bracelets. I presented the spear to my friends as I filled them in on the Femorian pirate attack. By the time I mentioned the story about the Milesians and the island killing storms, I was hyperventilating. I'm not sure why I kept the bracelets a secret.

Síofra put her arm around my shoulder. "We're sorry we didn't get here sooner. If it weren't for Mac Tíre, I'd still be arguing with Biróg. She can be so stubborn. When he arrived and realized you'd disappeared, he knew exactly what had happened."

"How did you convince Biróg to help you?" I said.

Mac Tíre removed a canvas sack from his saddle and tossed it over his shoulder, letting his horse graze. "It's a story for another time, but she owes my family and therefore me a huge debt. I just called it in." He set the sack on the ground, loosening the ties and spreading it open.

"Is that what I think it is?" Síofra asked, her eyes wide.

"That depends," Mac Tíre grinned. "What do you think it is?"

Right on cue, a worm slithered out of one of the eye sockets, and another from the mouth. "It's the Dullahan's head," I said in awe.

Síofra and I moved in for a closer look. "No one escapes the Headless Horsemen," she said.

Mac Tíre anchored his hands on his hips. I half-expected him to crow. "When people say something can't be done, that makes me want to try harder. I suspect we all have that in common."

I smiled, and I noticed Síofra did as well. "Tell us how you captured his head."

"It was easier than I thought. This Dullahan was quite the talker, which proved his undoing. He told me a Goblin alliance was forming. While he was bragging how easy it would be to control the humans and defeat the Sidhe, I threw my cape over his head, which meant he couldn't see where we were going. Since the Dullahan's horse also doesn't have a head, it was confused, reared, and the Dullahan and I fell off its back. After that, things happened fast. The horse raced into the woods, I tied up the Dullahan's body and took his head."

I nudged the head with my toe. "The head is glowing."

Mac Tíre closed the sack. "He's upset. A Dullahan never fails. He's quiet now, but a few minutes ago he claimed an army of Headless Horsemen would track me down and tear my arms and legs off if I didn't return his head to his body. There was also mention of feeding my eyeballs to fish."

I grimaced. "We get the idea. Did he mention any details about the alliance?"

"Only that whatever they're planning will happen on Samhain Eve."

"Mac Tíre," Síofra said with a false sense of calm, jerking her head toward the horse grazing nearby. "What is the Pooka still doing here? You said as soon as he brought us here, you'd send him away."

"We need him."

"You know he's a Pooka, right?" Síofra said. "Shape-shifting monster. Appears around this time of year. Leads unsuspecting humans hundreds of miles from their home. Most feared fairy in Ireland."

Mac Tíre rolled his eyes. "Most feared? Really, Síofra? Try wrestling with a Headless Horseman. Besides, he promised he'd behave."

I admit I wasn't excited about having a Pooka around, but Mac Tíre seemed to have the situation under control and we had bigger problems. This was as good a time as any to explain out my plan. Plus, it would distract Síofra. Her hands were balled into fists and she looked like she wanted to punch Mac Tíre.

"I saw John Dee," I blurted. "He was on the sky-ship that attacked Mug Ruith's workshop. Finn was right. He's headed to Dublin."

"Then it's already too late," Síofra said. "It will take days to reach him."

Mac Tíre motioned toward the Pooka. "Not necessarily."

Síofra crossed her arms over her chest. "Absolutely not."

Chapter Sixteen

Síofra was outvoted.

All three of us rode on the back of the Pooka, who raced so fast through tall grasses and over well-traveled roads that it felt like we were flying. The Pookas' reputation for speed had not been exaggerated.

Mac Tíre had said he knew exactly where the Femorian pirates would go to repair their sky-ship, *Goblin Bones*. We reached the Sidhe port city on the South Coast in a blur of screams, intermingled with shouts of joy.

Síofra and I did the screaming.

Mac Tíre, the cheering.

As promised, as soon as we'd reached our destination, Mac Tíre released the Pooka, which made Síofra breathe easier. For my part, I'd grown fond of him. He wasn't so bad.

The dock was like nothing I'd ever seen before, which was understandable since ships were anchored both to keep them from drifting away on the outgoing tide as well as from floating into the clouds on a gust of wind.

Síofra looked as pale as new snow. She marched over and punched Mac Tíre in the arm. "I still do not like Pookas. Any plans on how we are going to join the crew of a pirate ship without being eaten?"

"A few, but it means you and I find John Dee's

ship before we're discovered. Grace, you stay here. You look too human."

"What do you mean I look too human? I am human." They didn't answer my question. They'd already gone on ahead.

I'd accepted this quest for one reason. Everyone thought it was to save my parents. That was only part of it. I'd thought it would be easy. Find and return the Book of Invasions. Break the spell. Prove to my father I was worthy enough to crew on one of his ships.

Now, all of that seemed like the dream of a silly girl. Much more was hanging in the balance. If I failed, my father and his crew wouldn't be the only lives lost. My mother, my home, the villagers, and all the people I'd grown up around would be at risk. Then there were the people I didn't know and probably would never know. If the Goblins gained control, the destruction was impossible to comprehend.

It started raining. Actually, it had never stopped. Only the intensity changed. Right now, the rain was serious as a storm moved in. Men standing in line didn't seem to mind the weather. Times were rough, even in the magical realm. Hopeful crewmembers were too focused on getting a job on one of the ships than complaining about rain.

Mac Tíre explained another reason why so many were here was that Femorian pirates didn't care about a person's qualifications. No one had to list the ships they'd sailed on whether they could handle themselves in a fight, or if they thought they'd get airsick. That was because life expectancy on board a Femorian pirate ship was three months. Less for a gunner, because the cannons were unstable and kept backfiring, killing or injuring anyone close by. The other reason was that if a gunner missed his target too often, the captain would pitch him overboard.

Needless to say, it was difficult getting volunteers. As a result, captains took everyone and anyone, and if they needed additional crewmembers, they kidnapped them.

I wish I could say the practice of kidnapping was used only by Femorians, but unfortunately, it was a common practice in the human realm as well. I hoped my father had never resorted to those tactics. I'd never asked, and I knew it was because I was afraid of the answer.

"Which ship is yours?" A boy who looked around nine or ten appeared next to me, holding hands with someone I assumed was his twin brother. Their faces and clothes were caked in mud as though they'd been swimming in puddles, which for boys that age wasn't really that unusual. But their features were what was unusual. They had the roundest, brownest eyes I'd ever seen and were so large they dwarfed their mouths and noses.

I couldn't tell if they were human or magical, but I was learning that, even with my mother's ring, sometimes I couldn't tell. For example, Síofra looked exactly the same as she always had. If she had wings, they didn't show.

The boy who'd spoken blinked and looked like he was about to cry. No doubt wondering why I kept staring.

He was scared, and I was being rude. I couldn't blame him for being afraid. I was too. If I knew about the whole life-expectancy prediction, I was sure he did as well. It took courage to reach out, and I'd ignored him.

They might have been even younger than I'd first thought, maybe as young as six or seven. I smiled and spoke softly. "I haven't been assigned a ship." I wanted to ask about their parents but worried how to approach the topic. The sad truth was that as a result of wars, disease, and famine, Ireland was filled with orphans.

His brother stuck his thumb in his mouth and concentrated on making circles with his toe in a mud puddle.

I knelt until I was at their level. "My name is Grace. What's yours?"

The boy who was the more vocal of the two wiped his nose with the back of his sleeve, smearing more dirt over his face. "I'm Connor." He jerked his thumb toward his brother. "He's Ronan. He doesn't talk much. The man who brought us here promised he'd help us find our mother if we signed on as cabin boys."

My heart ached for him. "Where's your father?"

"We haven't seen him in a very long time." Connor glanced toward the dock. "We should go now. Our ship is leaving." He reached for Ronan's hand. Their expressions turned so hopeful, I almost broke.

I glanced around, for the first time really looking at those who stood in line. Maybe Mac Tíre had exaggerated the danger. I only needed a quick glance to determine my theory was a wishful dream. When I was wrong, I was very, very wrong.

A short distance away, a creature flipped the hood of his cape back. I turned Connor and Ronan away, hoping they hadn't seen him. The man—I assumed it was a man—had one eye shaped like an egg in the center of his forehead. Instead of hair, there were snapping, hissing snakes. The man yawned, and even from a few feet away I could smell his breath. It smelled like he'd been snacking on dead things.

I ground my teeth together to keep from screaming and scaring Connor and Ronan. I took their hands in mine. I admit it was as much to calm myself as it was to comfort them, and I ventured another look around.

Big mistake.

Standing next to the snakehead man was a creature with broad shoulders and a normal head. I eased my breath out slowly. His profile didn't look unusual. That was a start.

He was at least one body-length taller than my father. Although his nose was a little bigger than normal, his other features didn't set off any warning bells. His face was weathered like other seaman I'd seen on my father's ships. I took another calming breath. I'd overreacted. One really creepy monster didn't mean the whole dock was crawling with them.

Then he shrugged off his cape. Instead of one arm on each side of his body, he had two. I must have squeezed Connor and Ronan's hands a little too hard because they both yelped and tugged on my sleeve.

"Sorry," I mouthed.

Connor inclined his head toward the four-armed man. "I'll wager he can really climb the riggings fast."

I patted Connor on the head and nodded, knowing if I spoke aloud my voice would squeak like a mouse. I saw monsters. He saw a really cool rope climber. Go figure.

After that it seemed that wherever I looked, I saw another sailor more frightening than the last. I remembered Bíróg mentioned magical creatures from all over the world were entering Ireland. What if it wasn't just to seek asylum but to join the Femorians in a war against the Tuatha and humans?

Stopping the Femorians was more important than ever, but I had to do one thing first. I had to get Connor and Ronan as far away from here as possible.

****

"Move along." The order boomed from the deck of the ship. "We leave on the next gust of wind."

The sailors grew restless. They'd been quiet until now, but the order seemed to break the spell. They shifted around, looking at those beside them as though assessing the competition. A fight broke out between two men who looked like the snakehead guy's brothers. Another fight started with men who had heads that resembled goats. Goat-men butted sheep-headed men until a giant leveled them both with a club. Instead of quieting the crowd, it lit the fuse.

"We have a problem." Síofra said, coming from around a corner. "Good news: we found the ship. Bad news: Mac Tíre said it is ready to lift off." Then she noticed the twins. "Why are you talking to the children of a Selkie?"

"Connor and Ronan are not Selkies. They're human." I lowered my voice. "Someone tricked them and brought them here."

"They're still seal cubs," Síofra said, matching my hushed tone. "The question is why are they here? Femorian captains never allow them onboard. It is too dangerous. Manannan, the Lord of the Sea, is especially protective of Selkie cubs. Because more often than not, they're his children and anyone who harms or mistreats them risks death. Manannan sends waves as high as the clouds to bring down a sky-ship he suspects has a seal cub onboard."

"What's a Selkie?" Ronan said, speaking for the first time. "Is it a bad thing?"

Síofra cupped Ronan's face, giving him one of her warm smiles. "Being a Selkie is a very good thing, little one. You are one of the protected. The only question is why you and your brother are here."

****

Cannons exploded the air, followed by a puff of smoke. *The Goblin Bones* was leaving. Mac Tíre, Síofra, and I grabbed the children and ducked out of sight.

An assortment of both men and monsters pushed their way up the gangway. Someone screamed as he was shoved into the water. A shot was fired into the air, followed by the command for order. It didn't slow the chaos. The next shot was fired into the chest of a one-eyed giant. Illuminated in shadows was a young man. He was so reed-thin a sharp gust of wind could have blown him off the dock. His features were pinched, and it looked like he was talking to someone.

John Dee.

I left my friends and kept to the shadows as I crept toward John Dee. I would have found him by scent alone. He smelled like Grogoch mud. The odor marked anyone who had tried to sneak into the castle by swimming across the moat. I made a mental note to thank the Grogochs if I ever saw them again.

John Dee stood under the light of a lamppost near a stack of crates. The Book of Invasions was open. Because the pages were made from parchment, they crinkled as he turned each one with care. The letters were in an even, bold script and the artwork in the margins drew my attention as I edged closer.

Celtic symbols, swirls and circles glowed with vibrant color made from gold and silver leaf, green coaxed from buckthorn berries, red cinnabar, yellow saffron, and blue from crushed lapis lazuli stones. Horses, rabbits, and foxes either raced through meadows or looked out from behind trees or standing stones.

"Ah, Grace." John Dee's voice cracked along the edges like the pages in the Book he held and caught me off guard. "The Goblins did not believe me when I told them you'd be a problem." He glanced toward my sword. "I see you even have *Sea Pirate*. That confirms I was right about you."

I closed my hand around the hilt of my blade. He was talking about the Goblins as though they were allies, not kidnappers. Our friendship had clouded my opinion of him. "You were the one who tried to blow up the castle."

He shrugged. "You had to be stopped."

His words reflected what the tutor had said. I shuddered. John Dee was not who I had thought he was. I had wanted to believe he was a pawn, not someone moving the chess pieces. "You have to return the Book."

"I will do no such thing. The Goddess Epona foretold of your coming." His voice rose higher, shriller. His eyes glowed with an inner fire. "Two queens will rise. One by sea. One by land. I cannot allow that to happen. I will serve only one queen and she is yet to be crowned. You have to die."

I didn't know whether to laugh or scream. In addition to charting the stars in order to foretell a person's future, John Dee liked to interpret legends and writings hundreds and thousands of years in the past. There was a high probability he'd misinterpret Epona's words.

He traced a finger along the frame of the illuminated page. "Epona goes by many names. In Ireland she is the Great Queen Macha, one of the three war goddesses of the Morrigan. The raven rides with her to eat the souls of those she kills." The shadow of a grin gave me a glimpse into a dark soul. A place he'd kept well hidden. Until now.

He was mad. Mac Tíre and Síofra were right to question whether reasoning with him would work. I switched tactics. "If I don't return the Book in time, people will die," I said.

"Ireland is doomed anyway. She's been invaded many times before and will be again. She is Europe's closest known port before the Americas and her position is strategic, making her a rich prize. Everyone wants to possess her. The Book is a guide. No one can prevent the next wave of invaders. My goal is to assist the conqueror and earn a place in history."

"With all due respect, I doubt Epona meant me."

"There is no mistake. If you live, you will rule the seas."

"You are mad," I said. "The Femorians will destroy Ireland."

"Not destroy. Remake. When I present this treasure to Henry VIII's daughter, Elizabeth, I'll earn a permanent place in her court."

His selfish statement caught me off guard. At Oghy

U he had stated that knowledge should help people, not be used as a weapon.

"John," I began, forcing my voice to remain calm and reasoned. "Elizabeth is only a child. When her father dies, her brother Edward will be king. England will never give the throne to a girl. The Femorians have tricked you."

The lines around his mouth tightened. "I have foreseen Elizabeth's future in my star charts and it is entwined with mine." He paused. "As is yours, and like ivy winding around an oak tree, we will all prosper if we hold a common goal."

"Ivy is a parasite."

He frowned, closing the Book. "You do not understand. This is our chance at immortality. The star charts are clear. Elizabeth's father, sister, and brother are too weak to carry out this grand plan. Only Elizabeth has the courage and strength to propel England to greatness. Elizabeth will be queen. She will defeat the Spanish and French, and because I helped her, I will be known as the Queen's Sorcerer and will wield unlimited power."

Reasoning with a madman was like pushing water uphill with a fork, as Mary would say, but I had to try. "Spain and France are rich and powerful. England can't even pay her bills. You're misreading the stars. Besides, and this is a big one, foreseeing the future is considered sorcery, punishable by death. England burns or hangs witches. She doesn't reward them."

"She does if they are useful."

"Even if what you say is true, how can these stories in the Book help England? They were written down four or five hundred years ago from oral legends that were thousands of years old."

He chewed on one of his fingernails and it was then I noticed it was bleeding. Worry lines creased his brow, making him look older than fifteen. John Dee might speak with confidence, but he was worried. "Elizabeth is the key."

"Elizabeth is a child," I repeated.

"A child whose deepest desire is to rule now, not wait until her father dies. Beware. One day you will need her as a friend."

"You can't believe the Femorians." I pressed. "They are using you, filling your head with hollow promises. Elizabeth's mother was beheaded because the Privy Council said she was a witch. If anything, Elizabeth wants to survive, marry a prince of Spain or France and bring about peace, not engage in sorcery. Whoever is advising you is using you in a dangerous game. Don't do this."

"All aboard," the order rang out from *The Goblin Bones*. Ropes holding the ship to the dock released as the anchor rose from the sea. Sails billowed out and snapped in place as they caught the wind.

John Dee gave a desperate glance toward the powerful three-masted war ship as it rose into the sky. "I have to leave." He held my gaze in a vise-like grip. "Come with me," he said suddenly. "The stars say your future in Ireland is uncertain. Many paths are open. Join King Henry VIII's court. Share in my accomplishments and help me hold onto power." He sounded young and for a moment uncertain.

"I'll write my own future, not be tethered to yours," I said. I grabbed for the Book. He was strong for someone who looked as bony as a starving bird.

We both held onto it until our knuckles shone white with the strain.

"Epona's prophecy must not come true," he said. His voice sounded desperate.

His expression wavered like an image reflected in a pool of water. Without warning, he pushed me to the ground and jumped onto the ship's deck. I hit my head against one of the crates as I fell. My vision blurred.

The Goblin Bones cleared the dock and disappeared behind a shroud of clouds as gray as death.

Chapter Seventeen

I awoke to someone shaking me until my teeth rattled. I guessed it was Mac Tíre, as Síofra held a torch so near my face I felt its warmth.

"She's awake," Síofra announced.

Behind her stood Connor and Ronan, their expressions as full of concern as my friends.

"Are you all right?" Mac Tíre asked.

I pushed the torch away from me and stood nodding. "John Dee has the Book of Invasions," I said, feeling guilty. "He is also insane."

"You will get no argument from me," Mac Tíre said.

I dusted off my clothes, gazing in the direction I'd last seen his ship. "He believes the Femorians are taking him to England so he can turn the Book over to Elizabeth. We have to catch him before he reaches Dublin." I turned toward Mac Tíre. "Can we use the Pooka again?"

"He vanished at the first sight of the sky-ships. Afraid he'd be captured."

"A horse is of no use on a ship," I reasoned.

Síofra whispered close to me so the twins wouldn't hear. "Not as crew. As food."

My stomach roiled. "Then we borrow a ship."

A smile spread over Mac Tíre. "Borrow. Good word. A ship docked an hour ago." He nudged the twins. "They call the ship *The Selkie.*"

Connor and Ronan's grin were wider than Mac Tíre's. Apparently, while I was unconscious, the twins had embraced their Selkieness.

Mac Tíre continued. "The crew and captain are on shore leave and left their ship unguarded. I checked around. Because *The Selkie* is so small, they weren't concerned that anyone would steal…er…borrow her. She might be small, but she's sleek and built for speed. Perfect for our needs. We won't need a large crew."

"What are we waiting for?"

"Captain. Crew. A miracle," Síofra said.

"We can help," Connor said. "Our father told us we'd make good sailors."

Ronan smiled for the first time. "Grace will be our captain." His voice trembled as though he weren't used to speaking.

I was touched by their confidence, but my experience had been watching my father, not giving orders. "I've no experience. I'd run us to ground."

"Then it is good we are sailing the ship in the sky, not over the water," Mac Tíre grinned. "I will be the gunner."

I shivered. Cannons misfired. Exploded. I was about to protest, but Síofra had her own concerns.

"You told me you blew up the last ship you sailed on," Síofra said.

"An accident. Not my fault. So, do we borrow *The Selkie* or let John Dee and the Book fall into the hands of the Femorians?"

****

Through the pouring rain, *The Selkie* looked like the runt of a litter of kittens. Despite the approaching storm and the size of the ship, Mac Tíre looked almost as excited as when he had ridden the Pooka. I had to admit I was too.

The twins were a big help. They found a crew they swore we could trust as long as we paid them well, never turned our backs on them, and slept with one eye open. According to my father, the same was said of human crews.

There were two of the four-armed men, a dozen Grogochs, and a creature that changed form when he was nervous. One minute he was a horse, the next a man, and the least useful of all, a rabbit with really long ears. Whenever anyone asked to see the captain, we changed the subject. All except Ronan, who kept calling me Captain Grace.

Commands to weigh anchor and hoist the main sails set the crew into motion. Rain poured down like a waterfall after a spring thaw and the wind boiled the waves into foam.

Everyone had a task. The four-armed men climbed the riggings so fast they were a blur of arms and legs, exactly as Connor had predicted. Síofra directed the Grogochs to batten down the hatches and cargo, while the shape-shifter helped Mac Tíre secure the cannons and gunpowder. I stood at the helm, my hands on the wheel, holding on so tight my fingers ached. We needed a captain and in the end no one else wanted the job. I had trouble holding a thought. My heart pounded as loud in my ears as the thunder overhead.

Mac Tíre caught my gaze and grinned. He understood.

We were sailing into unknown dangers. We faced capture. Death. Instead of heading out to sea, we would soar into the sky like a giant bird. The odds were that we would fail. And yet, we both couldn't wait for the adventure to begin. I didn't know if I was afraid of heights, but I figured I was about to find out.

Chapter Eighteen

"*Goblin Bones,*" Ronan shouted over the storm from his perch on the mizenmast.

We'd been flying for over an hour with visibility near zero. We could only see a few feet in front of us. Once in a while, a wave rose high enough to brush against our hull. We kept on course, hoping Dublin was John Dee's destination.

Lightning crackled over the night sky as Ronan swung down from the rigging and landed at my feet. He nodded a quick greeting to Mac Tíre.

When I met Ronan a short time ago, he'd been timid and had spoken barely a word. Being on this ship had changed him. Even more remarkable, he and his brother now looked like they had aged four or five years. Their features were more defined and their shoulders broader. They walked with the confident swagger of seasoned crewmen, which confirmed Síofra's suggestion that because they were Selkies, the twins drew their strength from the sea. I was glad they were here. We'd needed all the able-bodied seaman in this storm when we encountered *Goblin Bones*.

I lifted my spyglass. John Dee's ship was silhouetted in the glow of another round of lightning. Their captain looked human, but looks were deceiving. The crew was an assortment of men and monsters. John Dee was nowhere in sight. Hiding below deck was my guess. Their warship was three or four times the size of ours. A killer whale against a cute harbor seal. Our only hope was to outmaneuver her.

"Stand by sheets and braces, coming up on the wind," I shouted. The wind filled out the sails and wood creaked under the added stress. "Prepare all cannons."

If I could position the ship so our cannons could make a high point shot to the stern, we'd take out the mast and officer's quarters and demoralize the crew. I'd seen my father use that tactic before. It worked with humans. I wasn't sure how a goblin crew would respond or how my crew would react with me as captain, but I was about to find out.

I took a breath and spun the wheel.

As smooth as cream poured over warm pie, the ship angled toward the new direction. Excitement surged through me. Father often said that a ship recognized its true captain. Until this moment, I'd never believed him. I'd thought it just another tale of the sea.

With newfound confidence, I bellowed orders. "All guns standby. Wait on my command."

Wind lashed against the hull and rain poured from the sky as we closed the distance. As I'd hoped, the size of our ship proved to hold the advantage. Despite her appearance, she was a well-made, sturdy, and faster than the wide-bodied *Goblin Bones*.

My heart hammered in my chest. "Prepare starboard guns. Standby on port." My voice wobbled on the last word. Mac Tíre assured me all the cannons were in working order, but I still worried. We wouldn't know for sure until they were fired.

I took a deep breath, willing strength into my words. The crew looked to the captain for courage. A weak captain, my father said, instilled distrust and fear. I dug deep, channeling the strength of the sea below and the sky around me. My voice drowned out the clap of thunder.

"Fire starboard guns."

Mac Tíre gave a nod of approval. He lit the fuses on the two cannons on the starboard side. Síofra and Connor stood by the guns on portside, waiting for more orders. The fuses Mac Tíre had lit made contact with the powder.

Cannonballs shot through the air, followed by a plume of smoke. They rent holes in the clouds as they sped toward their target. We held our breath.

A direct hit.

My crew cheered and I swear I saw Mac Tíre do a summersault.

Wood splintered on *The Goblin Bones*. Screams tore the cold night air. Rocked by the concussion, a few of the Femorians' crew were thrown overboard. Waves rose up to greet them and dragged them to their deaths. The plan had worked. I didn't hesitate. We needed to get off another round before *The Goblin Bones* had a chance to respond. The wind was helping, filing out our sails, and increasing our speed.

"The Femorians are turning their cannons toward us," shouted both Connor and Ronan from the mainmast.

A break in the smoke confirmed their fears.

"Hard to starboard," I shouted.

****

The Selkie leaned to starboard, trying to avoid attack. The maneuver came too late. A cannonball grazed the side of our ship and dropped into the inky blackness. The crew gave a collective sigh of relief when they realized it hadn't broken through the hull.

"Reload starboard guns. Standby port cannon. Jib around their stern." I snapped out orders in rapid succession.

Each one of my orders was met without question. I didn't know if I looked older like Ronan and Connor, but being on the ship built my confidence. I ordered the crew to change the position of the ship in order to keep the enemy guessing our next move. My crew sped over the riggings with ease and repositioned the sails for the difficult maneuver. The ship responded as though she were as excited as we were to prove she was ready for the challenge.

"Prepare the cannon for broadside." The Femorians were well-trained and reloading. If we didn't take the shot now, we might not have another chance. "Fire port cannons."

Síofra and Connor didn't hesitate. They lit the fuses. Connor had managed to stay clear, but soot covered Síofra's heart-shaped face and smudged her bright clothes. But she shared the same grin as we all had. Whatever happened, we were in this together.

We waited.

Another direct hit.

The explosion took out the enemy's aft deck. Men and monsters flew through the air. Their expressions reflected their disbelief and fear.

Another report of enemy cannon fire thundered through the chill air. This time their aim was off, and the shot fell wide.

We let loose another volley.

Water churned far below, but the sea was calmer.

More watchful than angry. I had the weird feeling it was waiting for the outcome of the battle. "Position cannons so that the first shot falls short and the next long, then reload."

"Master plan, Captain Grace," Mac Tíre shouted with pride through the thunder of wind and rain. "They'll be afraid to maneuver for fear our guns will hit their target."

When the smoke cleared, *The Goblin Bones* listed to the port, its sails were shredded, and its hull resembled a skeleton's rib cage, more bone than flesh.

A chant rose over *The Selkie.* "Captain Grace. Captain Grace. Captain Grace."

Ronan swooped down from the rigging, his chest puffed out like a rooster. "Now, we finish them."

I nodded, fighting back a grin. I was as excited as my crew, but we couldn't forget our goal. "Prepare to board. Capture John Dee alive."

****

Swinging from a rope was as much fun as it sounded.

One hand held *Sea Pirate*, the other, the rope. Mac Tíre made it to the enemy deck before me and engaged the Femorians. His shape-shifter friend was close behind, as were the Grogochs. The Grogochs told us we'd earned the right to learn their names. The tallest of the four declared their names were Larch, Mallow, Tansy, and Pinks, but neglected to say who was who. Ronan and Connor *arghed* like real pirates as they swung alongside me. Only Síofra stayed behind, and she didn't look happy about it.

As soon as we were on board, a one-eyed Femorian giant arched his sword and tried to lop off my head. I rolled out of the way, coming up behind him. Disoriented, he turned left and right, unable to locate me. I took the advantage and kicked him overboard, then ran to help my friends.

"Have you seen John Dee?" I shouted toward Mac Tíre, and then motioned to the Grogochs to secure the helm.

"*The Goblin Bones* is breaking apart," Mac Tíre yelled back as he defeated a four-armed man. "I think John Dee is down below with the captain."

I had a bad feeling. Captains usually didn't hide while their ship was under attack. I stepped across a body slumped over the staircase and ventured into the bowels of the ship. The companionway leading to the captain's quarters was littered with broken crockery, discarded weapons, glass, and splintered wood.

The door swung open on squeaking hinges, inviting me inside. Cowering in the far corner near the window was John Dee. The lone window was open, and the shutters banged against the outside hull.

"Where's your captain?"

John Dee gazed toward the lone window in the cabin. "The captain said he couldn't be captured."

I thought about telling him that his captain was a coward and that he should have stayed behind to fight. The concept wouldn't matter to John Dee. He wouldn't understand loyalty.

"Give me the Book." I held out my sword, not sure if I could use it now that we were face to face. John Dee looked younger, more vulnerable. More like the student I'd come to know as my friend rather than a traitorous, untrustworthy thief.

He'd wrapped his arms across the Book and

hugged it against his chest as though he meant to protect it with his life. "One last chance," he said. "Come with me."

I advanced slowly. "We've captured your ship. You're our prisoner. It's you who is coming with us. I promise we won't hurt you." To prove my point, I sheathed my blade and held up my hands to demonstrate I wasn't hiding any other weapons.

He shifted his gaze toward the window again and moved in that direction. "I'm not worried. No one will harm me. I have foreseen my future."

He was as easy to read as the book he held. He would attempt escape. He'd jump to his death rather than hand over the Book. "John, your ship is breaking apart. If you want to live, we need to leave. Now."

My voice of reason seemed to break him from his delusion. Still clutching the Book, he rose and allowed me to lead him to the deck. *The Goblin Bones* looked like a hollowed-out shell. Few of the bones remained to hold it together. My crew was back onboard our ship, releasing the ropes that tethered the two ships together.

Mac Tíre had remained behind, waiting for me. "The Femorian crew refuses to leave. They're waiting for their captain."

"John Dee said their captain jumped overboard," I held onto John Dee, who seemed in a trance. "Do they realize their ship is doomed and if they stay onboard they will all die?"

"Most of them are the *Marbh Bhee*. They're already dead."

"Captain," Ronan shouted from across the space that divided the ships. "*The Goblin Bones* won't last much longer."

Mac Tíre slung John Dee over his shoulder and grabbed one rope while I held onto the other. We swung over the abyss. As soon as we landed, Connor severed the last remaining ropes that tethered us to *The Goblin Bones*.

We pulled away from the enemy ship just as it broke apart and disappeared into a bank of storm clouds. Lightning flashed, and then silence.

Chapter Nineteen

The storm rumbled around us as we moved farther and farther away from the demise of *The Goblin Bones*. Ice-laced rain pelted down in a never-ending torrent, as though it could go on forever. We secured John Dee in the hold, feeling that it was the safest place for him and the Book of Invasions. There were those onboard who threatened to do him harm.

John Dee had never let go of the Book and every time anyone tried to take it from him, he went wild. We decided the best thing to do was wait until we reached Oghy U and let someone there deal with him. I couldn't bring myself to put him in irons. Besides, we were in a flying ship. Where could he go?

I expected he would be cowering in a corner as he had before. Instead, he looked like he was enjoying himself. He was looking out the small porthole into the night.

"The stars see everything," he said in awe. "They never disappoint. Do you ever wonder what they're thinking?"

I bit back my opinion on whether or not inanimate objects could think. "I have come for the Book."

Calm washed over his expression as he turned toward me. "Things are not always what they seem. I have to leave." His gaze flickered in the direction of the porthole. It was just big enough for him to fit through.

The realization hit me with the power of exploding cannon fire. "Are you mad? If you jump, you'll die."

My attempt at reason fell on deaf ears. Perhaps when it came to John Dee, it always had. I dove for him in the exact moment he leapt toward the porthole and grabbed for the Book. This time I was prepared. I wouldn't be fooled by his weak appearance. I held on.

The Book flopped open in our joined grasp. My fingers tightened around part of the spine and the brittle pages, while John Dee did the same on his end. We wrestled for control.

The spine of the Book cracked. It was tearing apart. The vibrant golds, blues, greens, and reds swirled off the illuminated pages, and spiraled together in shades of slat gray to molten black.

I held on tighter.

John Dee glanced toward the Book and then the porthole, as though debating which he valued most, the Book or freedom.

Without warning, he released his hold on the Book. When he let go, it took me by surprise and everything happened at once. I lost my balance and I fell to the ground as he dove through the porthole.

Stunned, I rushed over, trying to grab for him, but I was too late. John Dee plummeted toward the sea. He disappeared into a blanket of soot-gray clouds.

Mac Tíre burst into the hold. "Did you see it?"

I slumped against the wall, clutching the Book against me in the same way John Dee had moments before. I nodded, processing my emotions. John Dee had betrayed us, yet he'd also been my friend. I pushed away from the wall. "He jumped to his death."

Mac Tíre shook his head slowly, as though trying

to solve a puzzle. His lips tightened.

Foreboding descended in the small space that separated us. I swallowed, dreading his answer. "That's not the reason you're here. What did you want to tell me?"

"*The Goblin Bones* has returned. Ronan spotted the ship off our starboard side. I thought we defeated them too easily. The ship reformed and looks bigger than before. John Dee didn't jump to his death. He was rescued."

Chapter Twenty

Mac Tíre's words haunted me. *The Goblin Bones* had returned.

But we had the Book. We had the spear of Fionn mac Cumhaill which we hoped would defeat Lord Aillén, the Fire Lord. I'd given both the Book and the spear to Mac Tíre for safekeeping. We should be celebrating. We had four days to reach Clew Bay before Samhain Eve. Plenty of time.

When a new storm appeared that made the last one look like a spring breeze, we all knew we were smart to postpone our celebration. Especially when the Grogochs wouldn't stop calling it a bad omen.

Mac Tíre came up alongside me, his face a troubled mask. "The Grogochs believe the storm is worse."

"I agree, but attempting to land when we can't see through the dense cloud cover isn't the answer. Instead of water or a nice meadow, we could land the ship on rocks or on the top of a mountain."

"The Grogochs suggested a solution. It involves Síofra and something about an enchanted castle built by one of her parents. Except Síofra doesn't know it exists."

"What don't I know?" asked Síofra.

Mac Tíre hesitated, not sure how to begin. "How much do you know about your mother and father?"

"You mean the ones who abandoned me? Those parents?"

"Technically, it was your mother who left you. I do not think your father knew, or at least that is what the Grogochs claim."

Síofra narrowed her gaze at Mac Tíre. Anger flickered behind her eyes. "And how would they know?"

Mac Tíre glanced my way. It was obvious he didn't want to bring up a painful memory, but we were running out of options.

I dove in. "The Grogochs claim you have a castle."

All four Grogochs, Larch, Mallow, Tansy, and Pinks, shuffled up to Síofra and turned their great green eyes toward her. There seemed to be a silent communication between them because Síofra's expression changed from confusion to agitation and back to confusion all in the span of seconds.

She sighed. "I have a castle. Except it's enchanted. I'm the only one allowed entrance. And my friends," she added.

"Of course, it's enchanted," Mac Tíre said, crushing his arms against his chest. "I'll wager that if anyone gets too close they will be turned into a frog."

"Cockroach."

"Even better."

"I'm teasing," Síofra said.

Mac Tire stormed off to help prepare the ship to land. I nudged Síofra on the shoulder. "You weren't teasing."

She sighed. "The truth is that I don't know what to expect. Being turned into a cockroach is the least of our worries."

****

The decision made, we headed in the direction of Síofra's castle. It wasn't a hard choice. The storm was raging as though it was a two-year-old with a temper tantrum. If we didn't land, we'd break apart, and unlike what had happened with *The Goblin Bones*, no one onboard *The Selkie* knew a rebuilding spell.

The wind shifted. It felt different this high off the ground, as though it knew we didn't belong in its domain and was trying to frighten us away. The tactic was working. The wind tossed us like children's toys or drove us into clouds saturated with rain.

Shouts to batten down the hatches, snap to, and secure all lines were familiar phrases I'd heard on the voyage with my father to visit my brother in Galway when I was twelve years old. There had been a storm then, too. Waves had dwarfed the ship. Men had prayed to their Christian God. But with no end in sight, they had turned to one of the old Irish gods: Manannan Mac Lir, Lord of the Sea, and Protector of Sailors.

For some reason that I still don't understand, I hadn't been afraid, which annoyed my father. I'd told him everything would be all right if we changed course and veered along a northwesterly direction, catching a warm current. He'd given me an odd look and told me the storm was my fault. He said it was bad luck to bring a girl onboard and that he should never have listened to my mother. Our conversations went downhill from there.

Then for some inexplicable reason, he took my advice.

When his ship was safely out of the path of the storm, he stood in silence while all his crew, from seasoned seaman, to the cabin boy, had congratulated me on my skill at reading the wind and currents. I was a natural born navigator, they said. Blessed by the gods. Destined to become a great captain. Ballads would immortalize my name. The words and praises continued, except it was my father's praise I wanted, not theirs. His expression of complete fear had stunned me into silence. Why was he so afraid?

If I could pinpoint a time, an exact moment when our relationship changed, it was on that day. We'd barely spoken since, and he never allowed me on one of his ships again.

Waves rose as high as the ship, bringing me back to the present. Rain lashed against me, chilling me to the bone. I gripped the wheel tighter. Salt water combined with the salty taste of tears. I swiped both away, not wanting my friends to notice. I needn't have worried. Mac Tíre and Síofra were on deck making sure everything was tied down and the twins were tending the sails.

The wind increased and ripped the sail off the main mast. Its ropes snaked through the air as though alive. Several of the four-armed men clung to the mast as the pole swayed.

The main mast snapped in half like a dried twig. The four-armed men clung to the top half, screaming as the mast cut through the sky and into the dark void below. Another surge of wind tilted the ship on its side. Cannons broke free from their restraints, rolled across the deck, and crushed into crewmen, pinning them against the railing.

"Look out!" Mac Tíre shouted. He dove out of the way as another cannon rolled past, smashed into the side, creating a gaping hole.

Exactly like the voyage with my father to Galway, I knew what we had to do. Síofra reached out to me as I rushed past.

"Where are you going?" Her face was a frozen mask of fear. For as long as I'd known her, she'd never shown extremes of any emotion. Not happiness. Not sadness. In the last few days, she'd made up for lost time.

Surprisingly, this was the first time since I'd begun my quest that I wasn't afraid. I knew if I was to act, it had to be now. And I knew the direction that would take us to safety.

Another blast of cold air spiraled from one side of the ship to the other, dragging another crewman overboard. The ship rolled as though climbing a wave one moment, then plummeted toward the sea in the next. Lightning lit up the sky and split the clouds in two.

The ship wouldn't last much longer.

****

We were down to one sail.

Ronan and Connor replaced the damaged one and hoisted a new sail in its place, all while we spiraled to the ground. When the sail caught the wind, I knew it was our one chance. Just like in the ocean, currents wove through the air like silk threads in a finely woven tapestry. The trick was knowing which one to take. Trusting my instincts, I spun the wheel, catching a current in an easterly direction.

We needed to slow down. We were moving too fast. Landing at this speed, either on land or water, would break our ship apart and likely kill everyone onboard.

My crew was in frantic mode, climbing the riggings, holding on for dear life. The ship was dropping like a rock.

Síofra, on the other hand, looked at peace. She peered over the railing and raised her arms.

The clouds parted like curtains on a stage and exposed the bluest lake I'd ever seen. The wind died down to a gentle breeze, and the rain turned to soft mist as the ship slowed. Below us a castle rose to meet the clouds; its beauty made the one in the city of Tir Na nÓg look like a mud hut.

Chapter Twenty-One

We landed in a quiet cove, shrouded in a silver mist that sparkled as though alive. The ship was in worse shape than I'd thought. Gaping holes peppered the hull and it looked like a monster had taken a bite out of our portside. Ronan and Connor said they'd help the Grogochs with repairs, but this was as far as they could go. I wanted to stay as well, but Mac Tíre looked anxious, and Síofra looked so jumpy I thought she'd dive overboard and swim to shore. That was a terrible idea, since I knew she couldn't swim.

Usually Síofra was content to follow behind. Not this time. As soon as we anchored, she ordered a boat lowered. We reached the shoreline in silence. With us rushing to catch up, she forged a path through the underbrush. It was as though she knew exactly where to go.

Mac Tíre came up beside me. Since we'd landed, he'd been as silent as Síofra. "Síofra's mother abandoned her, and her father and relatives stood by and did nothing. If it were me, I'd hold a grudge until the earth erupted in a ball of flames." His voice was tentative, as though testing his words.

What he said seemed to catch him off guard, as though he hadn't meant to say so much. A shadow crept over his features.

"Mac Tíre, are you all right?" The more I got to

know him, the bigger a mystery he became.

"Lost in memories. Never a good place." He rubbed his hand over his face as though trying to wash away his thoughts. "Did Síofra ever tell you if she knew the identity of the human child her mother took in exchange or the reason her mother left her?"

The idea that a parent could kidnap someone else's baby created a hole in my heart I doubted would ever heal. When I shook my head, he continued.

"Well, it's been my experience that the Sidhe's reasons are always selfish," he ground out in response.

I had a feeling he wasn't just talking about Síofra.

"Síofra's stopped," he said.

We reached the end of a path that was an open field shrouded in more mist. I wondered if Ireland produced anything except the clinging, damp stuff. At least this mist was sparkling.

Síofra looked at us both, and I could tell something was bothering her.

"My mother gave me a castle," she announced with a pinched-faced expression that indicated she considered the gift on the same level as a bowl of wiggling maggots.

I walked over to her and gave her a hug. I knew how she felt. Every time my father returned from one of his voyages, he brought back gifts for my mother and me. We always made a big deal about how excited we were and made sure we told him how generous he was and how much we liked the gifts. My mother and I never said anything, but I knew she felt the same way I did. We didn't want gifts. We wanted more time with him.

The mist lifted with each step we took as though

someone knew we were approaching. The castle's stone walls were painted with gold and caught the morning sun, and the watch turrets were polished silver and disappeared into fluffy clouds. Not to be outdone, a curtain wall made from amethysts encircled the grounds and protected the keep inside. Of course, an enchanted castle was not complete without twin marble tower gates flanking the drawbridge and studded with diamonds.

For all its beauty, Síofra gazed at it as though she wanted to tear it down with her bare hands. "The Grogochs said my mother conceived the idea for the castle while traveling in Germany. When I was little, I was sick most of the time. Maybe my mother knew that would be my fate and that was the reason she left me." Síofra's voice shook, struggling to control her pain. "My mother believed hiding the castle once it was constructed would be the biggest challenge." Then Síofra did something extraordinary. She smiled. "Building it proved more difficult."

I disliked seeing my friend in so much pain and tried to lighten the mood. "What, no magic wand? No spells?"

Síofra's smile widened. "According to the Grogochs, Mother tried to use all the magic at her disposal. Nothing worked. The most she conjured was a rickety old stable that kept collapsing. She was forced to hire workers."

"Your mother must have hated that," Mac Tíre said.

Síofra laughed. "According to the Grogochs, it almost drove her mad, but that wasn't the worst of it. Once the castle was completed she tried to move in her belongings, but the drawbridge wouldn't open for her and she had to scale the walls to get inside. Once she was settled, the doors kept locking, fires refused to stay lit, candles blew out and food disappeared. She tried stocking the cellars with food but each morning all the supplies would be gone."

"It's as though the castle didn't like her," I said.

Síofra let out a short laugh and nodded. "The best part was when she installed a boiler, with hot and cold running water, like the one King Henry VIII has in his gardenrobe in London. She wanted to take warm baths in her chamber, but the boiler cracked and flooded the upstairs. The final straw was when the toilet that emptied into the moat backed up."

"The castle is cursed," I said, feeling a little anxious. I was glad it didn't like Síofra's mother but wasn't sure how I felt about entering a vengeful castle.

"Maybe it's not a good idea we go inside." Mac Tíre added, mirroring my thoughts.

"It will not harm us. The Grogochs told me my father is a druid. He was furious when he discovered she'd given me away. When he learned about the castle, he conjured a very specific spell. The castle reflects how my father feels about my mother. He shut her out of his life for what she did to me."

****

Síofra was in such a good mood, I decided not to point out the obvious. If her father knew about her, why hadn't he tried to find her? Instead, I focused on the castle.

If I thought the outside was a confection out of a candy lover's dream, the inside took my breath away. The courtyard was the size of a small village, devoted to the Celtic gods and goddesses. Everywhere you looked there were statues and gardens with ponds, winding streams, and fountains. Inlaid tiles, sea-shells and gem stones, covered the walls, retelling the stories of Ireland. Its defeats as well as its conquests. All the myths and legends I'd ever heard or read about were on display. But was I the only one who noticed that the grounds were immaculate? A place this size would require hundreds of workers, yet it looked deserted.

"I'll say one thing," Mac Tíre said, glancing toward the tiled roof. "Your mother knows how to build a castle.

"She's a member of the Sidhe," Síofra said with a brittle tone. "They surround themselves with beauty."

We walked on in silence. Mac Tíre's expression was masked, while I kept an eye on the gargoyles, half-expecting them to pounce. I swore I saw one wink.

The keep was in the center, and we headed toward it. Despite what Síofra had said, I wasn't sure of our welcome. One thing I'd learned on this quest was to expect the unexpected.

As soon as we drew near, the doors opened on their own. Inside the Great Hall, a long trestle-style table was placed in the center piled high with food and delicacies. Fires roared in hearths on either side of the room, and waves of comforting warm air chased away the cold. Somewhere a harp played.

I shivered and rubbed my arms, remembering childhood stories that all seemed to begin this way right before the monster jumped out and ate you.

The table was set for three, which gave me pause. I didn't think Síofra's mother had anything to do with the preparations because of the whole spell-thing. So, who was responsible? Síofra's father? The Femorians? After the reappearance of *Goblin Bones*, I didn't want to discount any possibility. We knew nothing about her father, other than the fact that he was a druid and druids were like everyone else. Some were good, and some were evil.

My stomach rumbled, responding to the smell of food. I couldn't remember the last time I'd eaten. Logically, if the castle didn't like Síofra's mother, we had nothing to worry about. The castle could be our friend. My mind did that spinning thing, which either meant I was trying too hard to make sense out of something that would never make sense, or I was hungry and therefore rationalizing. I concentrated on the positive. Someone knew we needed to eat and rest if we were to be at our best when we met the next challenge.

What drew my attention was that each place setting was different. One was gold, complete with gold plates, forks, knives, and a matching goblet. The next setting was silver and glowed so bright, the firelight reflected over its surface like a mirror. The third was a combination of both gold and silver, with Celtic symbols in blue enamel decorating the surface.

Mac Tíre and Síofra didn't hesitate. Síofra sat down at the gold place setting and Mac Tíre the silver, as if they knew that's where they belonged.

I followed their lead, settling behind the third place setting. There were great platters of blue berries, blackberries, and cherries arranged next to soft and hard cheeses, walnuts, hazelnuts, and almonds, as well as breads still steaming from the oven and pitchers of foaming buttermilk. I reached for the buttermilk first, not realizing how hungry and thirsty I was until I took the first sip. The buttermilk was smooth and rich with just the right touch of honey.

"I'm not complaining," I said, "but when my parents have a feast, they serve roast pig, venison, chicken, or lamb."

Síofra heaped a handful of nuts on her plate. "We're in the land of the Tuatha. They don't eat meat."

Mac Tíre nodded with a mouthful of cheese and bread, and then pushed a pitcher in front of me. The pitcher was filled with a frothy dark liquid. He swallowed and wiped his mouth with a cloth. "It's called chocolate and was discovered in the new world by Hernán Cortés. The monks are studying why it is so popular in the new world. They claim it must have magical properties."

I poured myself a goblet and took a drink. Instantly, I felt invigorated, as though I'd had a nap or a good night's rest. "This is wonderful," I said, taking another sip.

Feeling satisfied, we settled beside the fire. Síofra curled up on a wool blanket and went to sleep. When she was breathing comfortably, Mac Tíre turned toward me.

"What is your story?"

I cupped both my hands around my chocolate. For some reason, his words were unsettling. "I don't have one."

He focused on the flames as they curled around the squares of peat and wood. "Everyone has a story. Everyone has things they're hiding."

"I'm here to recover the Book, break the sleeping spell, and find my father. Isn't that enough?" Even as I said it, the words sounded hollow. When I had begun the quest, I had been so clear on what I had to do. Now I wasn't so sure. "What about you?" I said, changing the subject. "All I know is that you are on your own."

"Interesting that you mention the Book of Invasions first and your father last."

"You avoided my question."

"As did you. Old habit, on my part. What is your excuse?"

I took another sip of chocolate. It was cold. I set it aside. "My father and I aren't that close anymore. And my mother..." I reached for the chocolate and finished every drop.

Mac Tíre stretched out in front of the fire. "You and I are not that different after all. My relationship with my parents is complicated as well." His expression closed, as clearly as though a door had shut. He rubbed his eyes with the heel of his hands and yawned. "At least your father didn't kick you out of your house."

Chapter Twenty-Two

I awoke with a start. Mac Tíre and Síofra were asleep by the fire. Flames rolled gently in the hearth, giving off both fragrance as well as soothing warmth. Sometime in the middle of the night, someone had covered us with wool blankets. After Mac Tíre had made the announcement about his father, he'd closed back up and I hadn't pressed. The hurt in his eyes said it all. I considered him my friend. As much as I wanted to help, he wasn't ready to share. I wondered if any of us were.

If you put words to an emotion, it becomes real. Adults said that was the first step toward healing, but it only worked if you were ready. I knew I wasn't, and I suspected neither was Mac Tíre or Síofra.

I shook off the overwhelming impulse to curl back under the blankets and sleep. Something was wrong. I could feel it in the air, like the approach of a storm. Everything was too perfect.

Keeping the blanket wrapped around my shoulders, I rose, trying to shake my unease. I slung Mac Tíre's knapsack containing the Book over my shoulder. I didn't want it out of my sight. The table had been cleared of all the food, and fresh place settings laid out for the morning meal. Three stacks of clean clothes were folded on a bench against the wall. I knew without checking that they would fit Síofra, Mac Tíre, and me perfectly, as though John Dee's father, who made clothes for nobles in England's court, had taken our measurements.

The castle wanted us to feel at home. It had the opposite effect. We were being watched.

I clutched the blanket tighter as I rounded a corner of the Great Hall. At the end of the corridor was a room shaped like a half moon with floor-to-ceiling windows. Pale morning light rested on a small square table with two chairs positioned on opposite sides. On the table was a game board, like the one Liam and the goddess Bridget had been playing at Oghy U the day my life turned upside down. I remembered the game was called *Fidchell*. Three chess pieces were placed in the center squares, while other chess pieces were positioned around them.

"We're surrounded." Mac Tíre yawned, coming up alongside me and stuffing cheese and bread into a cloth sack.

"Does that mean that Liam is winning?" I asked.

Mac Tíre nodded toward the window. "I have no idea who's winning the game. I was talking about what's going on outside. The castle is surrounded."

I headed over to the windows and used the end of my sleeve to rub the film off a pane of leaded glass. "Are you sure? I can't see anything out there. The stupid mist is too thick."

"Trust me. They are out there."

"They?"

Síofra approached, wrapped in an oversized blush-pink blanket. "Isn't that cute," she said with a smile, nodding toward the game board. "The chess pieces in the center look just like us."

****

Síofra was right. The chess pieces in the center looked exactly like us. I wrapped the blanket tighter around me, about to ask her if this was some sort of Sidhe welcoming tradition. The Irish were famous for their hospitality, and law mandated that you offer a stranger a warm meal, lodging, and entertainment. The Irish language even had a phrase for it, *céad mÃ-le fÃ¡ilte*, which means, 'a hundred thousand welcomes.'

A chess piece on the *Fidchell* game board moved.

The figurines were carved to resemble the Femorians onboard the *Goblin Bones*. The piece that moved had one eye, four arms, and an angry expression. There were a lot more Femorian-looking pieces, as well as a horse with a headless rider, and a few that looked like the Walking Dead. On opposite sides were two game pieces carved to resemble a druid and a goddess.

As though moved by invisible hands, the army advanced one square at a time, as though taking turns. First, a chess piece moved from the goddess' side of the board, then one from the druid's.

I glanced outside again. If anything was out there, it was difficult to see through the mist and pouring rain. I turned back to the board, remembering Liam's words, "The world watches." He'd said the words as though the game he and the goddess played had real-life consequences. True, the pieces were shaped realistically. Was it more than a representation of people, monsters and other beings? Were they really controlling us like a puppeteer controlled his puppets?

"Mac Tíre, do you believe Liam knows we're here?" I couldn't voice what was on my mind. To suggest that we might be under someone else's control was too disturbing. My fate was my own to control.

Mac Tíre ran his hands through his mane of hair. "Liam could be one of the players. There are thirteen *Fidchell* boards, each with its own druid and opposing god or goddess. The locations of each are a closely guarded secret. I hate games. We should just move the pieces. See what happens."

Síofra looked closer at the druid. "Only those appointed can play," she said. "This one does not resemble Liam. He is older, with curly hair and blue eyes." Startled, she straightened. "The druid looked at me."

I wanted to believe she'd imagined it. "It is only a game," I said with more hope than conviction. I also wanted to mention that the druid looked like Síofra, but that didn't make sense.

Mac Tíre glanced toward the window. "We're surrounded. Just like on the game board."

"How many of the enemy are there?" I asked.

Mac Tíre grinned. "Planning on fighting our way out of here? I like how you think, Grace." His grin widened. "But there are hundreds of them and three of us. I have another idea."

Without warning, he snatched our pieces at the same time and moved them outside the circle of Femorians.

"What have you done?" Síofra said in a high-pitched shriek.

"I saved the day."

"You moved the pieces. Why did you move them?" Her voice rose in panic. "You changed the rules."

"I do not like rules. I thought you knew that about

me." He turned to leave, but his feet looked like they were stuck to the marble floor.

I tried to take a step but with the same result. "I can't move either." I looked over at Síofra. She was as stuck as we were. To her credit, she didn't say I told you so.

The game board vibrated.

Mac Tíre drew his sword. "Get ready."

****

And as fast as you could say "I hate games," we were standing in a soggy field of mud, pummeled by rain and wind and facing a Femorian army. Behind them was a battalion of Headless Horsemen. I didn't see any Walking Dead, but that didn't mean they weren't out there. The configuration of the enemy mirrored the placement of the chess pieces on the board.

We stood in a circle with our backs out, probably sharing a common thought. *We are so dead.*

The Femorians were as frozen in place as we were and looked like they were waiting for orders.

It was the oddest sensation. We were surrounded by bad guys who carried knives, swords, or clubs in each hand. But everyone was standing still as though waiting for the signal to charge. If I could read their thoughts, I suspected they were thinking how they would kill us when they got their chance. If they all attacked at once, it wouldn't be that difficult. We were outnumbered one hundred to one.

Then the strangest thought came to me.

"Are they waiting for the opposing player to make the next move?"

Síofra gave a slight shrug as if to say that sounded

as good an answer as any.

"Speaking of moving," Mac Tíre said, "has anyone tried to…you know…move?"

I tried, but my feet wouldn't budge. Instead of glued to the floor of a castle, they were sunk in spongy earth. I shook my head. "Still stuck."

"Me too," Síofra said.

Mac Tíre just grunted.

"Well, we can't just wait here," I said.

Síofra said, "We don't have a choice. We can't move until it's our turn. That's how the game is played."

Mac Tire rolled his eyes. "I changed the rules. Remember?"

"Mac Tíre's right," I said. "Maybe the real reason we're all stuck is that the players are trying to figure out who has the next turn."

"They're immortal," Mac Tíre said, "which means we could be here until our bones turn to dust."

It was Síofra's turn to roll her eyes. "Leave it to a guy to make a dire situation sound worse."

"Except you know Mac Tíre's right. We need to break this spell. Síofra, you mentioned that the chess piece didn't look like Liam. The Grogochs said your father was a druid. Is it possible that your father is playing this game?"

Síofra turned away. "When I was younger I made up stories to explain why my parents abandoned me. My mother was the fairy queen Fand and my father was the warrior, Cuchulainn. They left me on your doorstep because they had to defend the fairy realm and it was too dangerous for me to stay with them."

I squeezed her arm gently, not sure what to say.

There were times I'd wished my parents were different than they were as well.

Mac Tíre shrugged. "I understand why you hoped Cuchulainn and Fand were your parents. Fand is considered the Irish version of the Greek Aphrodite and Cuchulainn is compared to the Greek demigod Achilles. But that doesn't mean they would have made good parents. Like Achilles, Cuchulainn had his share of weaknesses. The major one was that he was unfaithful to his wife, Emer." Mac Tíre's voice trailed off as he turned toward me, encouraging me to finish the story.

I nodded. "I know the story of Fand and Cuchulainn," I said. "Fand, in her sea-bird form, was flying with her sisters, joined together with a silver chain. From the shore, Cuchulainn threw stones at them, hitting their wings. They turned back into human form and attacked him. Fand was a kind person at heart and felt so bad about what they'd done, she healed him. He also felt remorse and offered to help her defeat her enemies."

Mac Tíre jumped in. "He should feel bad. Cuchulainn bragged that he was a protector, not someone who threw rocks at enchanted creatures. Not exactly hero behavior."

Síofra laughed. "Enough. I get it. You two are as subtle as Mary when she claims she's made extra apple pie and needs us to help her eat it. I may never know who my parents are or why they left me, but I couldn't have asked for a better adoptive family than Grace's. I knew I was loved."

I looked over at Mac Tíre and he gave a slight nod of approval. We'd had the same goal. Being famous or beautiful didn't make a person a good parent. My father was a powerful warlord and pirate. He'd also had numerous affairs and never bothered to keep them a secret. I had at least one half-brother, probably more. By betraying my mother, he'd betrayed me. It seemed being unfaithful to the person you'd vowed to love was common in both the human as well as the magical realms.

I pushed the pain back into its hiding place, and like Síofra, I knew that I was loved.

"For sake of argument," I said, clearing my throat, "let's say your father is a druid." I rushed on with my idea before Síofra could offer any objections. "Síofra, there was a druid on the game board. You said yourself it didn't look like Liam. I didn't want to say anything earlier, because it seemed too weird, but the chess-piece druid you said glanced toward you looked like you. What if your father is one of the players?"

"I'm listening." Síofra's voice sounded strained.

"Call out to him. Ask him to push us over, as though we were chess pieces. Mac Tíre lifted us off the *Fidchell* game board, so pushing us over shouldn't be that difficult."

Mac Tíre turned toward me. "Are you mad? Standing in the mud is bad enough. I don't think you'll like it when we are face down, and snow clouds are hovering above us. Winter is coming early. Soon this whole field will be covered in snow."

"I have a theory."

"That it's better freezing to death lying on the ground than standing straight up?"

I frowned at Mac Tíre before turning toward Síofra. "The Grogochs said your father cast a spell over the castle your mother built because he was unhappy about what she'd done to you. If this druid is your father, I'll wager he'll want to help."

"But what should I say?" Síofra asked. There was so much pain in her words that both Mac Tíre and I exchanged glances. I couldn't imagine how she was feeling.

I rested my hand on her shoulder. "Just ask him to help us. If this works, we'll have a few seconds before our bodies touch the ground. The moment you feel yourselves toppling over, start running."

Mac Tíre tightened his grip on his sword while Síofra drew in a deep breath of the snow-filled air, and I crossed my fingers for good luck. Síofra hesitated a few more seconds then shouted our request. For good measure she repeated it three more times.

I couldn't remember how long it had taken between the time Mac Tíre moved our game pieces and the time we'd ended up here. One minute? Two? Two and a half...

****

Snow swirled around us and the Femorians, settling on our shoulders, and transforming the muddy field to winter-white. It almost looked beautiful, if you could forget the whole freezing to death scenario.

When I started to think Síofra's father either hadn't heard her plea for help, or the idea was flawed from the beginning, we all toppled over at once as though someone had snapped his fingers and pushed us over at the same time.

I screamed "*run*," but Síofra and Mac Tíre didn't need any encouragement. They were already headed toward a corpse of trees. Following close behind, I plunged into the woods, thankful that the canopy of trees protected us from the snow.

Behind us, Femorians and Headless Horsemen were still stuck in the same position and cursing at the top of their lungs. Their prey was escaping and there was nothing they could do about it. But once we reached the woods, the rules changed.

Directly in front of us stood two Femorian warriors. Maybe they'd been late to the party, so they hadn't been included in the game of *Fidchell*. Maybe they'd opted out. Or maybe they were scouts. Whatever the reason, it didn't matter. They blocked our path, drew their weapons, and advanced toward us.

"Are we ready?" I asked.

"I was born ready," Mac Tíre's answered.

Síofra and I both shot him a glance, but she beat me to the response. "Are you kidding?"

He had a sheepish grin. "Always wanted to say that."

The Femorians charged, their weapons raised. One headed toward me, the other toward Mac Tíre. I was just glad we weren't outnumbered, but when my sword vibrated against the steel weapons of the Femorian warrior I battled, I changed my mind. They outweighed us by at least two hundred pounds. At least they were slow.

I used my size and agility to my advantage and ducked when my assailant swung his blade. Síofra thwacked him on his back with a thick branch she'd found. Confused, he roared as though not knowing which one of us to attack first. Not giving him the chance to decide, I sprinted around him, clipping him in the leg with my sword. He yelped and spun around with his weapon, but he looked like he was moving in slow motion.

Out of the corner of my eye, I saw Mac Tíre battling the other Femorian. It was hard to see who was winning.

A trumpet blared, ripping the air. Both Femorians jerked toward the sound. Dismissing us as though we were no more important than annoying insects, they headed in the direction of the meadow.

"That was strange," I said.

"I'll say," Mac Tíre said in disbelief. "They were winning."

Síofra tossed her branch in the bushes and dusted off her hands. "What do you think it means?"

Mac Tíre motioned us to follow him into the woods. "They're regrouping."

Chapter Twenty-Three

Thankfully, the snow had stopped, but it was still cold. A shooting star swept across the night sky as though pulled by the Death Coach and a team of black horses. I shuddered. Mary would say it was an omen. A week ago, I would have only half-believed her comment. Now, I was a full-on believer.

We'd walked for hours without encountering a single Femorian. We should have been relieved. Not only was the forest a goblin-free zone, it was devoid of wild life. No birds. No squirrels. No creepy-crawly spiders. Nothing moved, slithered or crawled.

We hoped the Femorians had given up. We knew better.

The Logan Castle was still a long way off, so we decided to rest for a few hours before making our push home. Síofra was taking a nap, and Mac Tíre had wandered off. We had time. Samhain Eve was tomorrow. Mac Tíre had selected the top of a large hill, the site of what remained of a castle. The roof was missing, and the walls scorched and crumbling and was a stark difference from the castle Síofra's mother had created.

Mac Tire insisted the location gave us the vantage point of the valley for miles around. I was concerned about the possibility of ghosts but too tired and hungry to argue with him. Ghosts were famous for haunting castle ruins or castles in general, for that matter.

He was unusually quiet, convinced that the Femorians, Headless Horsemen, and Walking Dead were following us. That made no sense to me. They outnumbered us. If they wanted us dead, all they had to do was attack.

I opened Mac Tíre's knapsack, pulled out the Book of Invasions and set it beside me. Food first. Reading second. I moved aside Mary's pouch of healing herbs and reached for the bread and cheese.

I broke off a corner of the bread and glanced over at the Book. Curious, I drew it closer. I hadn't had the chance to look at it since I'd taken it from John Dee. Illuminated pages were bound together between blood-red leather covers, and considering its age, it was in amazing condition. According to Finn and Mug Ruith, the reason there had been a shift in the balance of evil was that someone had ripped out sections of historical accounts regarding the Tuatha de Danaan.

Taking a bite of the bread, I thumbed through the pages, trying to figure out if any pages were missing.

I gazed toward the sky again. The full moon was only partially visible, and the clouds were thin and frayed, like the edges of torn silk. Mac Tíre had just returned and stood a short distance away looking relaxed, as though he didn't have a care in the world. I knew better. He was standing guard.

Síofra lay curled in the hollow of a tree, her arm tucked under her head like a pillow. She looked fragile and small. The only reason she'd come along in the first place was because I'd volunteered. Since childhood, we'd been inseparable. Síofra had a way of looking on the positive side and her example made me want to be a better person. I should have told her to stay behind.

Guilt washed over me. She looked like a gust of wind might brush her aside as easily as if she were a fallen leaf or petals on a flower. Mac Tíre, on the other hand, looked as solid and constant as standing stones. Fear was not a word in his vocabulary.

Trying to take my mind off my guilt, and the possibility that Mac Tíre was right and the Femorians were still hunting us, I moved over to sit opposite him.

He withdrew his sword from its scabbard. His scabbard was lined with sheep fleece and lay balanced across his knees. Next, he removed a flat stone from a velvet pouch that looked like two stones stuck together. One side was yellow-gray, and the other a cobalt blue. With long, even strokes, he used the stone to sharpen his blade. He was so calm it was almost disturbing.

"Mac Tíre?"

"Not hungry." He hadn't even looked up. He kept sharpening his blade as though he had all the time in the world.

"No, that's not what I was going to ask." Stalling for time, I hesitated and said, "Interesting stone." The look he gave me held such pain I pulled back.

His expression clouded over. "Ask your question."

"Why are you so sure the Femorians are hunting us?"

He jerked his head toward the valley.

Tiny pinpricks of light flickered below. If Mac Tíre hadn't pointed them out to me, I doubt I'd have seen them. I furrowed my brow.

"Campfires," Mac Tíre answered. "They are stealthy, I'll give them that."

I stood up abruptly to get a closer look. Mac Tíre

yanked me back down. "Do not give them a target."

I lowered my voice to a hoarse whisper. "How can you be so sure it's them?"

He resumed sharpening his blade. "You do not have to whisper. They cannot hear you. The wind is against them. But as to how I knew, that is easy. All the wild life in the forest ran for their lives. I've rarely witnessed such a universal panic. I think the trees would have uprooted themselves if they could. And then there was the smell."

"My tutor smelled like rotting seaweed and dead fish."

Mac Tíre gave a satisfied nod. "Multiply that by hundreds."

"But I didn't smell anything? I still don't." I must have looked as confused as I felt.

He heaved a deep sigh and straightened. "I have an unusually keen sense of smell. Eyesight as well. I can see as well at night as I do in the day."

Silence stretched out between us while I processed what he'd said. Mac Tíre looked like he was waging an inner battle. A few times he glanced over at me, only to look away when I met his stare. Was he saying he was a member of the Sidhe just because he had heightened senses?

I clasped my hands together in my lap. "Are you trying to tell me you think you have Sidhe blood, like Síofra? Because, not everyone who is good at something has a fairy in their blood-line. I never get lost, that doesn't make me Sidhe."

The shadow of a grin flickered over his expression, and then disappeared as quickly as it had appeared. "Perhaps, you are right, but you deserve to know my story," he said at last. "You have earned the right."

I pulled my knees against my chest, not wanting to say anything that would break the moment. He wore secrets like a cape, and I knew something about how difficult they were to shed.

He looked away. "I'm a wolf."

****

"A wolf?" I slid off the rock I'd used as a chair.

Mac Tíre grinned and helped me stand. "I seem to be the one who's always helping you to your feet."

Still feeling unsteady, I glanced toward him expecting to see…well, I wasn't sure what I expected.

He smiled when he saw the direction of my stare. "No pointed ears. No tail." His expression shifted, clouding over. "When I was younger, I was a lot like Finn. I could shift form at will, much in the same way Finn summons his wings."

Shifting into a wolf was nothing like fairy wings, but I decided not to press the point. I'd never had much contact with wolves, but stories didn't paint them as friendly. They ran in packs, raided our sheep herds, and kept to themselves unless confronted. Knowing Mac Tíre was a wolf punctuated how little I really knew him, or his world.

My legs buckled.

Mac Tíre caught me. I clung to his arms as he guided me over to the rock. "Thank you, by the way."

"Why are you thanking me?" Mac Tíre said. "I shouldn't have reacted so strangely." He gave me his characteristic grin, and I was glad I was still holding onto him as his eyes held so much warmth that I almost melted against him.

Still holding me, he said. "I knew you'd be

shocked. Most people who do not grow up around the Sidhe usually are. I'm thankful because you didn't back away from me."

"What did I miss?" Síofra yawned and walked toward us, picking up the Book and tucking it under her arm. "Are we under attack?"

"Did you know that Mac Tíre is a wolf?"

She looked toward me, then Mac Tíre, and then back to me. "It was his secret to keep," she said, in defense. "Not mine to tell."

They stared at me, gauging my reaction. Síofra was right. Sure, it wasn't everyday you found out that your friend was a wolf, but in the stories about them, there were also all the good things. Mother and father wolves were protective of their cubs and took turns caring for them. They were loyal to the members of their pack and mated for life.

It was my turn to grin. "You're a wolf. Síofra's a Changeling, and I want to be a pirate. We make a good team."

"And as a team," Síofra said walking over and setting the Book beside me.

"We should probably figure out our next move."

Chapter Twenty-Four

We huddled under the shadows of the ruins. Freezing rain had started to fall while storm clouds churned overhead. Lightning cracked and illuminated the clouds from behind, giving the illusion that they were on fire.

And as Mac Tíre had said, the Femorians and an army of Dullahans had us surrounded.

What was even more disturbing was that our enemy wasn't trying to stay hidden. They'd built their campfires higher as though they wanted us to know where they were. It spoke to the fact that they weren't afraid of us.

"They don't seem in a hurry to attack," I said, my teeth chattering together in the cold.

Mac Tíre blew on his hands. "The Fire Lord guards the Logan Castle and while his power grows, the Femorian's goal it to keep us here until after Samhain Eve. After that, it will be too late. The Goblins will rise, and the Fire Lord will be too powerful to stop."

Síofra sat down on a rock and glanced over her shoulder toward the campfires. "We'll have to sneak past the Femorians of course, but we have Fionn mac Cumhaill's spear. All we have to do is make it to Grace's castle before Samhain Eve, and get close enough to the Fire Lord to throw the spear into his mouth. We've got this far. How hard can that be?"

We all glanced toward each other and then burst out laughing, easing the tension until Mac Tíre said, "As Síofra pointed out, we first need to escape. I'll shift and hold them off for as long as I can, while the both of you head for the castle."

"You cannot," Síofra protested.

"Why not?" I said. "It's the perfect solution. It's a full moon, and Mac Tíre said the Headless Horsemen are afraid of wolves."

"Terrified, actually," Mac Tíre said with a smile. "Probably the reason they've enlisted the help of dogs. They think the animals will be a match for a wolf."

"Weren't wolfhounds bred to kill wolves?"

Mac Tíre looked like he was trying hard not to laugh, which I thought was a strange reaction. "Yes, they were. Except the Dullahan didn't bring wolfhounds, or feisty sheep dogs, or even the hardy Irish terriers, they brought along Irish Water Spaniels. Excellent at retrieving small game, loves to please, barks a lot." His grin widened. "Not a match for wolves. I guess the Dullahan thought one dog was as good as another. First time I've ever heard Irish Water Spaniels complain."

"You can hear their thoughts?" Butterflies, not the good, fun kind, but the frantic, oh-my-gods kind, started to flap their giant wings in my stomach. "Can you hear mine?" I sounded more frantic than I'd intended.

He shook his head. "Only animals."

Letting out a breath in relief, I continued, suppressing the urge to punch him in the arm. "I know we're outnumbered, but their army is in the valley directly below us. There's a big boulder overlooking their camp. A perfect spot for them to see you after

191

you've turned. You could stand or whatever wolves do. Howl. Snarl. Maybe some growling."

Síofra looked like if she were a teakettle, steam would have poured out her ears. "Tell her," she ground out.

"What am I missing? Is it painful to turn?" I knew nothing about the process. I'd seen Finn's wings appear out of thin air and he didn't react with so much as a groan.

"Painful? No. I mean, I do not remember. The last time I turned, I was a cub."

"Tell her," Síofra repeated. "You know it is not my place to tell another's story."

Mac Tíre glanced toward the valley as though he'd rather be fighting a hundred Headless Horsemen by himself. "My mother put a *geas* on me. Her parting gift. She said she was doing me a favor. Some favor. I ended up shunned by my father and his wolf pack."

Sensing my confusion, Síofra said. "A *geas* is a binding spell and takes many forms. One of the war goddesses had a crush on Cuchulainn, I forgot which one, but Cuchulainn being who he was, had just fallen in love with someone else. He turned down the war goddess' advances."

"He turned down a goddess?" I squeaked, knowing that couldn't be good.

Mac Tíre gave me a lopsided grin. "Not one of his wiser moves. In her raven form, the war goddess spied on Cuchulainn and harassed him whenever he went into battle. But by then he was a famous warrior and felt he could ignore her. One day she overheard him bragging that a *geas* was placed on him a long time ago and that it was powerless against someone like him."

I leaned closer. "Seriously? That didn't sound bright. What was the *geas*?"

Mac Tíre's grin had returned. "The war goddess had a sense of humor. Cuchulainn was nicknamed, Hound, after he killed a guard dog in self-defense by mistake and offered to take the animal's place until another one was trained. The war goddess created a *geas* that made it taboo for him to eat dog meat."

I grimaced. "So Cuchulainn couldn't eat dog meat?" My stomach churned like the first time I had seen fish heads simmering in Mary's seafood stew. I swallowed. "That sounds like an easy taboo to keep."

Mac Tíre looked as green as I felt. "You'd think so. The whole idea is disgusting. But there's more. If Cuchulainn ate dog meat, he'd die in battle. Good incentive to avoid dog meat, if you ask me."

"Except that by that time, Cuchulainn was a famous warrior," Síofra continued. "He could have anything he wanted and believed nothing could harm him. He'd survived battles and angry gods and goddesses countless times. He felt invincible. Immortal."

"Pride causes the end of more heroes than the sword," Mac Tíre said almost to himself.

Siofra nodded in agreement. "The goddess appeared in the disguise of an old crone one day when Cuchulainn returned from battle. She was roasting dog meat on a spit made from the branch of a Rowan tree. I think he knew exactly who she was. The stories say he was tricked, but I think he ate the meat in defiance. He died in battle later that afternoon."

We all fell silent. I glanced over at the Book of Invasions. Because it had been missing, warriors like

Cuchulainn were young again. Would they commit the same mistakes over again when they got older? Was that why they were so afraid?

"How does your *geas* work?" I said to Mac Tíre, feeling protective.

He was sharpening the end of a stick with his knife and seemed relieved to be drawn out of his thoughts. "Not as disgusting as Cuchulainn's, thank the gods, although death is still the theme. The gods and goddess aren't very imaginative in that regard. If I turn into a wolf, I'll die."

Grace shivered. "That's awful." She hesitated, not wanting to ask him what he'd done to bring down a *geas* that strong.

"The geas wasn't his fault," Síofra said, as though reading my thoughts. "Mac Tíre, tell Grace the whole story."

Mac Tíre leaned back and heaved a sigh. "I was just a young pup, but I knew my parents were not getting along. Dad was our tribe's Alpha leader and Mom was a druidess who claimed Dad promised he would give up leadership of the pack and come live with her in one of the cities of Tir na nÓg. There was a terrible argument, complete with flames and choking smoke. One minute I was a happy, fun loving wolf-cub, playing with friends and chasing squirrels. The next, I was human. She'd placed a *geas* on me and taken off. Hard for a son to follow in the leader's paw steps if the young pup can't turn into a wolf. Naturally, as I grew older, my Dad and I tried to kill each other."

"But how could he blame you?" I said.

"I think I reminded him of the mistake he'd made in marrying my mother. Wolves mate for life, and as long as she was still alive, he couldn't remarry. Unrest in the pack was building, and his leadership was challenged. Leaving seemed the logical choice."

The only sound was Mac Tíre's knife whittling the wood into a lethal point. No wonder he'd run away from home. I wanted to ask him if he'd ever tried to find his mother, but the pain in his expression told me there was still too much hurt and anger. In trying to get back at her husband, she'd cursed her only son.

"I will do it," Síofra said.

Chapter Twenty-Five

Mac Tíre and I both looked her, probably with the same puzzled expression.

"What exactly do you plan to do?" Mac Tíre asked with a touch of irritation in his voice. "If your idea is to confront the Femorian army by charming them with enchanted fairy-speak that will turn them into nice people, giving Grace and me a chance to escape…" He paused to take in a breath. "That's a horrible idea and doomed to fail. I forbid you."

Síofra pulled her hair back behind her neck and tied the curls with one of her ribbons. "For your information, I plan to turn into a giant. It should only take a short time." She made the statement as though she'd announced she was going to the market, not transforming into a monster. "And just so you know, wolf-boy, enchanted fairy-speak is a myth. Well…mostly."

"Hold on," I said. "You can turn into a giant?"

Mac Tíre had a different approach. "You've come into your power? When did it happen?"

"What are you two talking about?" I asked, glancing between Mac Tíre and Síofra.

Síofra avoided me as she took off her shoes and placed them neatly beside a tree. "It started about a week ago. It was raining, and I remember thinking it would be fun to be small enough to use a mushroom as an umbrella and poof I—was mouse size. I've only tried shrinking in size. But when I get smaller, my clothes shrink with me. Except for my shoes. Not sure why. I'm hoping the same thing happens when I grow taller."

I was still struggling with what I'd learned about Mac Tíre, but I hadn't known him that long, so it didn't bother me as much as Síofra's revelation. Síofra and I were best friends. We shared our secrets, or at least until this quest, I thought we had. This was yet another example of how little I really knew her and yet she knew everything about me. I pressed my lips together, afraid to voice my hurt feelings.

She continued as though sensing my discomfort, trying to make it right again between us. "Everything happened so fast. Before your mother gave you the ring that helped you see us in our true form, I thought you might…well, I guess I didn't know how you'd react to my new power. I kept silent. I was struggling with how to tell you when the castle was attacked and after that there never seemed to be a good time."

Mac Tíre was watching us. Or more precisely, he looked like he was gauging my reaction. I felt like this was another test. One I was failing. No one was as they seemed. Everyone had a secret they were afraid of sharing. But was knowing a person's secrets as important as the nature of their heart?

Mac Tíre was loyal and trustworthy. It seeped from every pore. Síofra was pure love. She saw the good in every living creature. I felt like I was still a work-in-progress, as Mary would say. One minute I was brave, the next a puddle of doubt. And yet, for all our insecurities and secrets, the three of us had formed a strong bond.

I couldn't think of the right thing to say, so I gave Síofra a quick hug. The tension between us evaporated. "Cool power," I said and realized I meant it.

Síofra grinned. "I'm still figuring things out as I go. Your mother was a big help. She'd told me something might happen close to my fifteenth birthday and that my power would offer a clue as to why my mother had exchanged me at birth."

I tried to process what Síofra was saying. "Did my Mother give any hint?"

Síofra looked away. "She wouldn't say.

Síofra reached for a chain around her neck and showed me a charm shaped like golden fairy wings. "When I told your mother I could change my size, she gave me this charm as a birthday present. She said if I change while I'm wearing the chain, the wings will grow or shrink with me."

"You will be a giant, scary fairy," I said.

"I know what you're thinking Grace Logan," Mac Tíre said, "and I won't allow it. It's too dangerous."

****

With Síofra's latest announcement that she could turn into a monster-like fairy still hanging in the air like a fat, gray rain cloud, she headed toward the shelter of the ruins to transform into a giant.

"Síofra. Wait," Mac Tíre said. "You can't face the Femorians and Dullahans looking like you do, only taller. When they stop laughing, they'll attack."

Defending my friend, I said. "I disagree. Giants are scary. Our enemy will take one look at Síofra and trip over themselves trying to outrun her."

"But what if they don't?" Mac Tíre asked

practically. "I mean, take a good look at her. What makes giants scary is not their size. It's much more. Cyclops and a majority of Femorians only have one eye. A Minotaur is over ten feet tall with the head of a bull, and the body of gladiator. Síofra will be a larger version of herself. Instead of scarring them away, she'll be a target." His expression was as clear as spring water. He took his protector role seriously. "Síofra, I know you're trying to help, but a giant fairy? If anyone can challenge the Dullahan, it has to be me."

"No," both Síofra and I said at the same time.

"Out of the question," I added. "You said you'd die if you turn into a wolf."

"It might take a while before I die."

"I keep telling you that it should be me," Síofra argued.

I rested my hands on my hips. "Stop it. Both of you. "We aren't leaving anyone behind. We have to reach the castle before Samhain Eve and kill the Fire Lord, and we're going together."

Síofra pulled her withered hand against her stomach. "Grace, please reconsider. I know if I turn into a giant, I can distract the enemy and give you and Mac Tíre a chance to make sure the portals to the Otherworld remain closed after midnight. Let me do this."

"Over my dead body," Mac Tíre said through gritted teeth. "That is a stupid plan. You are prepared to face an army of Dullahan and their minions knowing full well you won't survive. Something else is going on here and I have a good idea what it is. This is all about proving something to your mother and father. I have issues with my mine; Grace certainly has with hers.

There isn't a child born who doesn't. Those aren't good reasons to throw your life away. I'm with Grace on this one. No one stays behind."

"I am sure my mother had her reasons," Síofra said, as she sank onto the trunk of a tree.

"There's nothing wrong with you," I said, sitting down beside her and putting my arm around her. She didn't even hesitate. She leaned over and rested her head on my shoulder. Tears streamed down her face as though a dam had burst. I glanced over at Mac Tíre and mouthed a thank you. We couldn't let our friend risk her life while we ran for safety. I wasn't about to let Mac Tíre go it alone, either. Whatever happened, we were in this quest together.

"Mac Tíre, who knows about the *geas* placed on you?" I said.

"No one, besides you and Síofra. My mother vowed she'd never speak of it. Oh, and my father and his pack, but they are too embarrassed to tell anyone. Why?"

I smiled. "I have a plan."

Chapter Twenty-Six

For our plan to work, we had to trick the Femorians and the army of Dullahan to come to us.

Great leaders used the element of surprise. I was grateful that one of my favorite classes covered warfare and battles and what strategies worked and what didn't. Great leaders, I'd also learned, did not repeat failed strategies, nor did they knowingly send their troops into a battle where the enemy was prepared and waiting, without first having a plan of their own.

I joined Mác Tíre and Síofra on the boulder that overlooked the valley and the enemy below. We didn't see anyone with bows and arrows and felt safe for the moment. We'd guessed it was difficult for a Dullahan to notch an arrow on a bow-string while holding onto his head with one hand and the reins of his horse with the other. But we could see movement below as though they were planning an attack.

"That is a steep slope," I commented to my friends. "How long do you think it will take them to get here once they start the climb?"

"Hard to tell," Mac Tíre said. "Early tonight, I did a little reconnaissance at one of the camps and overheard the Femorian's horses grumbling. They are worried about being involved in an attack against me. If I'm killed, they fear my father's reaction. He's a big deal amongst the Sidhe community. Dad and I may not be on speaking terms, but I know him: he will take my murder as a challenge to his authority. He'll place the Dullahan and any creature involved on the endangered species list."

"Perfect. We'll use their fear," I said. "It fits into a battle plan idea called the *Fabius Strategy*."

Mac Tíre tilted his head in surprise. "I'm impressed. That's one of my favorite battles. It was between Rome's General Fabius and Hannibal Barca. Hannibal's the guy who crossed the Pyrenees Mountains and southern France with elephants."

"That was one of my favorites too." The admiration in Mac Tíre's expression made me blush. I averted my gaze. It was as though Mac Tíre was noticing me for the first time. I cleared my throat and continued. "As you know, Fabius' strategy was to avoid meeting Hannibal head on because he knew his men would be slaughtered. Fabius used the element of surprise and deception, and so will we." I motioned for Mac Tíre and Síofra to come in close and I whispered my plan, starting with the main objective.

Don't die.

****

Clouds passed over the moon and blanketed the stars as a murder of crows flew from the trees in the direction of the Logan Castle. I wasn't sure if we were being watched. Birds, especially ravens or crows, were little tattle-tales. I admit I couldn't tell the difference between them but after the story about the war goddess and Cuchulainn, I was worried.

I agreed with Mac Tíre that we had to do something about Síofra's appearance. We plastered mud all over her face, arms and clothes, and stuck twigs and branches in her hair. At a distance and in the dark, she would look not like a sweet fairy child but a scary monster. We hoped.

While Mac Tíre distracted the birds, Síofra headed toward a Portal Tomb to begin her transformation into her giant form.

Síofra wasn't sure how tall she'd grow since her experience had been concentrated on shrinking not growing. What she knew for certain was that her clothes or anything she touched would conform to the size she visualized. Síofra told us that the Sidhe could be any size they wanted. Small if they wanted to hide. Giant-size if the goal was to intimidate and human-sized when they interacted with humans. The theory that fairies were small because people had stopped believing in them was a myth. She also said that when the Tuatha and Femorians first came to Ireland they were all giants and that the land shook with the force of their footsteps.

Mac Tíre returned and settled into sharpening his sword again. I was starting to realize the task was more of a distraction than a need to make it sharper. "She'll be all right," he said.

I didn't know if he meant when she grew taller, or just in general. Either way, the words were comforting.

"It's this Book business that has me baffled," he confided. "The Book is more than a retelling of Ireland's invasions. If tampered with, it alters the past as well as the future. A dangerous tool or a powerful bargaining chip. When it was completed, a powerful sorceress constructed a wooden box from the remains of a fallen oak tree and cast a spell. Nothing can happen to the Book or the adults guarding it as long as it remains in its container. I'm not sure John Dee knew that when he stole it. Maybe, like us, John Dee is a pawn in the gods and goddess' game of *Fidchell*."

"We have to make this right." I said.

Síofra emerged from the ruins. She was over ten feet tall. Instinctively, I stepped back. She seemed older somehow, and more intimidating. For once, Mac Tíre was wrong. Even giants who looked as gentle as Síofra were scary. I was glad she was on our side.

I gave Mac Tíre the signal to light the torches to give the Dullahan a clear view of our new weapon. As planned, Síofra opened her mouth as though she was screaming, but it was Mac Tíre who let out a war cry that sent shivers down my spine.

In the next instant, he let out an entirely different sound. This one was the howl of a wolf.

I shivered and hoped he hadn't seen my reaction.

The hum of conversation below ceased as though on silent command. The Dullahan army turned their heads toward the hill and Síofra. The Irish Water Spaniels whimpered in response to Mac Tíre's call of the wild. The Walking Dead and Femorians either ran for cover or sank into the ground. Mac Tíre had said that unlike wolves, monsters didn't operate in packs. Dwelling in the Land of the Dead had taught them that every monster was on his own. Loyalty didn't exist. Most of them chose to flee rather than risk facing Mac Tíre or his dad's revenge.

As Mac Tíre had predicted, although a contingency of headless riders was trying to reach Síofra, their horses weren't cooperating. They stumbled over the rocky path and refused to go any farther. A few limped after twisting their legs on the uneven grade, while the others pawed the ground in protest. A few of the Dullahan dismounted and huddled in a tight group. They held up their heads, shouting obscenities at the horses. Their threats alternated between dire consequences if the horses didn't start moving and promises of extra treats. Nothing worked.

The Dullahan were so focused on their problem, they'd ignored Síofra.

Big mistake.

With Síofra's help, Mac Tíre and I rolled a boulder the size of an Irish cottage into place. She hefted it over her head as easily as if she were holding a seashell. Síofra paused as though calculating her aim, gave us a wink, and let out a very unfairy-like war cry.

The bolder sailed through the air in a perfect arc. It tumbled over and over in the air and slammed into the cluster of Dullahans. The enemy only had time to give a collective gasp before the boulder found its target. Heads flew in one direction, bodies in the other.

It sounded odd, if not impossible but I thought I heard the horses laugh.

Right on cue, Mac Tíre and I took off in opposite directions. The plan was to distract and confuse the army. With the Dullahans scrambling to recover, Mac Tíre went down one side of the hill and I the other.

I was almost there when I heard a roar: a sound halfway between the angry bellow of a wild boar and the deafening call of a bird of prey.

****

A monster out of a child's nightmare was headed straight toward me. Fifteen feet long with the head of an otter and the body of a crocodile, it wouldn't take long to reach me, and I couldn't turn back. There was no place to go. I recognized the creature from descriptions of bedtime stories.

The Dobhar Chu.

They lived around the water and this one looked grumpy. He'd probably missed its last meal. The Dobhar Chu was like a crocodile. It ate anything it could hunt and considered humans particularly tasty.

Heading straight for me, he swatted at low hanging branches that got in his way, as though the trees had done that on purpose to annoy him. I figured he'd been sent out as a scout with the promise he could eat anything he caught.

Mary said that when this type of goblin attacked, they put their head down and charged. Their prey was so scared, they didn't move. The prey stood perfectly still while the monster took a bite. It felt a lot like my encounter with the Mouldywarp. I had hesitated and let him gain the advantage. I'd learned my lesson.

I backed against an oak tree and I held out my weapon, Sea Pirate, while the Dobhar Chu pawed the ground and sniffed the air. I set my jaw and tightened my grip on my sword. Like the Mouldywarp, this monster needed food to live. That meant he could die.

He snorted and in the span of the next heartbeat, he charged, eating up the ground that separated us.

Twenty-five feet.

Fifteen.

Five.

At the last second, I leapt out of the way. The Dobhar Chu slammed into the tree. Dazed, he groaned and shook his head. He wasn't as disoriented as I'd hoped. In retaliation, he swiped at me. His claws scraped across my ribs. White-hot pain seared through me. Blood seeped through my shirt.

He sprang toward me again.

I barely had time to raise my sword as he leapt into the air. On his descent I clipped him on the leg with my blade. Blood flowed from his wound as he landed. It looked deep. He limped a little, then spun and snarled, baring yellow teeth.

I jumped for a low hanging branch and climbed out of his reach. He circled below, roaring in frustration.

He watched me warily. We each waited for the other to make the first move or the first mistake. I'd seen this tactic before on my father's practice field. It was all in the eyes, seasoned warriors would say. If your opponent's gaze flickered to one side or the other, it could signal that he was distracted. If you seized the moment, you increased your odds of survival. The Dobhar Chu looked focused. Determined. And really, really mad.

Growing impatient, he dipped his long neck to the side, set his shoulder against the trunk of the tree and pushed. As strong as he was, the oak tree had deep roots and it would take the Dobhar Chu a while to uproot the tree.

Meanwhile, Mac Tíre and Síofra were in the thick of battle. The clock was ticking. For our plan to work, all three of us needed to do our part and that meant I had to defeat this monster or die trying.

William had claimed Sea Pirate was a powerful weapon in the right hands. I figured this was the best time to test his theory. I leapt free of the branch, tucked and rolled as I fell, and landed in a standing position. The Dobhar Chu seemed surprised. Actually, I was too. Normally, when I'd tried that trick before, I'd landed in a crumpled heap.

I arced my sword over my head and turned in a circle, gaining momentum. A rainbow burst from the blade and enveloped me in multicolored light and power.

The Dobhar Chu put his head down and lunged.

I leaped into the air and drove Sea Pirate into the monster's head.

Chapter Twenty-Seven

The Dobhar Chu lay dead at my feet. His death-scream still rang in my ears. His eyes were closed, and blood oozed from the fatal wound. My sword arm ached from the impact, but I was alive.

I took a few calming breaths as I leaned against the tree, grabbing my wound. When the Dobhar Chu had sliced across my side with his claws, it had burned like someone had seared me with a hot fireplace iron. I clamped my teeth together against the pain and focused. The battle was not over.

"You have surprised us all," a woman said, her voice sounding like the noise Mac Tíre's whetstone made when he sharpened his steel blade. Not a good sound. She glanced toward the Dobhar Chu and then my wound.

I knew at once who she was.

"Hello, Cally."

The Banshee hung in the air like a spider's web that had been torn and battered in the wind. Her hair and garments were the same shade as those silken threads and appeared as fragile.

Her features kept changing. She looked young one moment, then old the next, then middle-aged, as though her real age were part of the illusion. The one constant was that she didn't look like she wanted to frighten me. Just the opposite. Her expression was sad, as though she regretted being the messenger of bad news all the time.

Cally motioned toward the sky and that's when I saw it.

A shadow arced over the face of the moon, heading in my direction. I gasped when it took form. A team of six horses drew a wheeled carriage through the clouds as though they were on a country road. Each horse wore bridles that shone brighter than the stars and their black manes and tails were braided with silver ribbons. The gilded coach looked like it was dipped in molten gold and studded with diamonds.

Gem-stones in ruby-red and firelight-amber framed the open windows and upper half of the door. Even from this distance. the plush interior looked like it was made from the finest black velvet. It reminded me of the King's and Queen's coronation coaches that John Dee said had drawn cheers and admiration from the villagers and townspeople from all over Europe.

But no one would cheer when they saw this apparition. The only emotion they would experience was fear. When it stopped, it picked up a passenger and drove them to the Land of the Dead.

"It's the Death Coach," I whispered, afraid to look away.

Cally nodded sadly. "I fear so. Once the *Cóiste Bodhar* is sent out, it never returns empty. The Death Coach's only purpose is to bring a soul back to the Land of the Dead for judgment."

My heart caught in my throat as I realized it was headed in the direction of Clew Bay. "My parents' castle," I said with rising panic. "You have to prevent it from landing."

A cold breeze rattled the bare tree branches like bones as the Banshee floated higher above me. "I cannot stop it once it sets out on its mission. My sworn duty is to prepare you. It is much easier when mortals know when their loved ones will meet death and are given time to say their goodbyes. When death is sudden and unexpected, those left behind spend the rest of their lives in regret and mourning. That is no way to honor the dead."

I couldn't debate the issue with an immortal. There was no way she could understand. I had known my grandfather was dying and I still regretted not having more time with him.

"You have to call off the Death Coach," I repeated.

It hovered overhead as though waiting for her signal. I sensed the Banshee was thinking it over, but in the end, she shook her head. I'd heard that sometimes the Banshee drove the carriage. Other times it was one of the Dullahan.

I gathered my courage. I'd been away from home for a week. Was it possible my father had returned from his voyage and lay dying? "Has it come for my father?"

The Banshee shifted in the air, gliding closer to me. "I do not know Dark Oak's fate." She paused, her image transforming until she looked almost solid. "The *Cóiste Bodhar* was sent to collect your mother."

I gasped. I felt trapped under water. I couldn't breathe. "She's asleep, not dead. If I make it back before midnight on Samhain…"

The Banshee looked older again, as though the weight of the world and all she knew had aged her. "Your mother stole something from us. When the *Cóiste Bodhar* touches ground and the doors open, she will be brought to justice."

With her words still ringing in my ears, she vanished.

When the Banshee disappeared, the wound in my side started to bleed again, as though she had momentarily stopped time. I pressed my hand again the injury. What could my mother have stolen that had caused the Tuatha to send the Death Coach?

****

Conveniently, the Banshee evaporated into thin air before she told me exactly what my mother had stolen. A ridiculous accusation. My mother had never stolen anything in her life. It was so like Cally to make a big announcement and then disappear. My imagination ran wild—everything from the standing stones in Galway to the gold monument to Crom-Cruaich.

First Mac Tíre appeared by my side, sporting a gash in his arm that was already healing. It must be the wolf-thing. Next, Síofra came into view. She'd changed back to her normal size and the minute she saw my injury, she began rummaging around in Mac Tíre's knapsack for the healing herbs Mary had packed. While she fussed and bandaged my wound, I filled them in on the battle with the Dobhar Chu, ending with Cally's announcement that my mother was a thief.

Being true friends, they concluded that my mother was innocent and Cally had a hidden agenda. I agreed wholeheartedly. We turned our attention to how to rescue my mother. Not only did we have to reach the castle before midnight to break the spell, but we had to make it before the Death Coach landed. No pressure.

For my part, I was in a thick fog of confusion. True, my mother had been more distant over the past few years. She missed Father and complained he was gone too much. But why would she steal from the Tuatha? None of it made any sense.

"We will reach her in time," Síofra said as Mac Tíre mumbled something about finding us a ride.

As he disappeared into the woods, I acknowledged Síofra's positive comment with a weak nod. I wasn't as sure. "You made a great giant," I said, trying to change the subject. "We couldn't have escaped without your help."

She gave a weak smile. "You and Mac Tíre did all the real fighting. All I did was wave my arms like a scarecrow caught in a windstorm. Pathetic."

"I meant it when I said we couldn't have escaped without you."

She rubbed her withered arm. "If we make it through, I've decided to try and find the Isle of Skye and visit the Shadow Islands. Una told me that was where she trained to be a Sidhe Warrior with the warrior queen, Aoife. I'm not sure how yet, but I'm not leaving there until they agree to accept me as a trainee. The location is a secret, however, and no one will tell me where it is. I know it's because they think I'm not worthy."

I didn't hesitate. I knew I'd taken the bracelets from Mug Ruith's workshop not for myself, but for Síofra. I offered them to her and squeezed her hand. Actions were the real test of friendship. "According to Mug Ruith, these bracelets will grant you safe passage to the training fields on the Isle of Skye's Shadow Islands. Once you're there, they'll recognize you as a great warrior."

Her eyes brimmed with tears, as she mouthed a

thank you and tucked them away just as Mac Tíre approached, leading three horses.

"They've agreed to take us as far as the hill overlooking Oghy U. and Grace's castle," he said, motioning to the horses. Then he looked first toward Síofra and then me. "What just happened?"

"Girl stuff," we both said at the same time.

Síofra turned her attention toward the horses and then narrowed her gaze. "Those…horses belong to the Dullahan and like the Dullahan, they are headless." She shuddered. "First you asked us to ride a Pooka. What is next? The flesh eating Nucklelavees?"

"We defeated the Dullahan, I'm pretty certain the horses are more afraid of you then you are of them."

"I seriously doubt that."

Mac Tíre mounted the lead horse. "We don't have a choice." He hesitated. "Forgot to ask. Before the Dobhar Chu died, did he scream?"

I nodded. "Loud enough to wake the Walking Dead." I thought he'd smile, but his expression darkened.

"Not good. He called for his mate."

Chapter Twenty-Eight

Síofra and I decided that taking a chance with the Dullahan's horses beat confronting an angry Dobhar Chu's mate. It was almost midnight and Mac Tíre informed us that she would track us down and kill us. A half otter, half crocodile out for revenge fueled our need to hurry.

I slung the knapsack containing the Book over my shoulder. "I think it's heavier."

"Magical objects have a mind of their own," Síofra said. "They take on the weight of their protector."

"And by now," Mac Tíre said nodding toward a lone raven as he flew overhead, "they've sold the information to our enemies that we're headed to the castle."

"I do not trust ravens," Síofra said, as though reading all our thoughts. "Their eyes look right through you. Very judgmental."

"The moon doesn't look right," Mac Tíre announced, mounting his horse. A halo of light circled the full moon, blocking out the stars. The sight was not uncommon, but given all that had happened, it was a bad omen. "A storm is brewing. We should get moving."

****

The number of the moon's halos kept multiplying in the same way circles increased when you skipped a

215

stone over the surface of a mirror-smooth pond. The meaning of the rings was the least of my worries, however.

When the moon reached its zenith, it would be midnight. Our only chance of returning the Book and breaking the spell was to kill Lord Aillén with the spear I'd taken from Mug Ruith's workshop. If we failed, everyone in the castle would die and the portal to the Land of the Dead would stay open permanently. Ireland would plunge into perpetual darkness and fear. No amount of sliced apples and hazelnuts on windowsills would keep the Walking Dead and Headless Horsemen away.

The Death Coach was above us matching our speed as though the Banshee wanted us to witness who it had come to claim. The Banshee was seated up front, holding the reins. I couldn't figure her out. Was she a friend giving comfort, or another Goblin ally? Bottom line—I didn't trust her completely. After all, she was one of the gods. Humans were pawns in their game of chess. Mortals thought of life in terms of years, the gods in centuries.

We approached the hill overlooking the castle and Oghy U. and near the area where the Herding Boys had attacked Síofra. A ruined tower stood guard, a reminder of the first visitors to Clew Bay. A week ago, I'd thought my biggest challenge was avoiding an arranged marriage or convincing my parents I'd make a good sailor. Preventing goblins from creating a never-ending Halloween had not been on my to-do list.

The full moon slipped behind wisps of dark spider-web clouds as though it were afraid. I knew how it felt as horses galloped toward us. Mac Tíre and I unsheathed our swords at the same time, while Síofra started to take off her shoes.

"Friends," a familiar voice shouted as he reined in his mount a short distance away. Síofra recognized Finn at once and waved a greeting. He raised his hands to prove he was unarmed. Behind him, Una rode a snow-white mare and Liam a silver gray. More students followed. Some rode on horseback, while others were on foot. They either had bows slung over their shoulders or held swords. All of them looked like they hadn't slept or eaten in days.

Mac Tíre edged his horse toward them, but I noted he hadn't sheathed his weapon. "The castle is freed, then?"

An uneasy glance was exchanged amongst the Sidhe warriors. "We escaped," Liam said. "We were coming to warn you. The Fire Lord has control of the castle as well as Oghy U."

Mac Tíre wore an expression of unmasked distrust. "Let me guess, we are walking into a trap." When Liam nodded, Mac Tíre slid me a glance and grinned. "We wouldn't have it any other way."

****

We formed a line on the crest of the hill. Bonfires blazed soundlessly. No sparks, no crackling sounds, just searing heat and stone-cold silence. The flames were an eerie, unnatural shade of white, like the color of sun-bleached bones.

"I wonder how many Femorians are guarding the castle and school?" Síofra asked, voicing what we were all thinking.

"We are going to die," Una added in a voice as low as a whisper. Her amber wings were tinged with gray, reflecting her concern.

Liam flipped off his hood. "By now the Fire Lord is aware you have the Book of Invasions."

Síofra, Mac Tíre, and I remained silent, avoiding Liam's penetrating stare. We hadn't told them we had the Book of Invasions. Had they assumed because we'd returned we'd succeeded? Or had the Ravens told them?

Perhaps the ravens had snitched. Síofra was right not to trust them. They spied for both sides with equal treachery. They owed allegiance to no one and didn't care which master they served. If they knew our plan and told the Femorians, we were walking into an ambush. But how had Liam found out about the Book? I knew my friends had added Liam to the list of those we couldn't trust.

"We'll need a way to breach the castle," Finn said, stating the obvious.

Mac Tíre looked away and muttered under his breath. "Duh."

"Too risky," Una pressed.

"We need reinforcements," Liam added in his superior voice. "Perhaps we can get word to Mug Ruith to send his siege inventions."

"No time," Finn shot back.

The trio argued back and forth until the sound reminded me of a swarm of angry bees.

Mac Tíre maneuvered his horse next to mine. Resting his arms on the saddle's pummel, he gave a quick nod to our new companions. "They're afraid."

"Aren't you?"

He narrowed his gaze down the valley for so long I thought he hadn't heard my question. When he looked over at me again his expression was calmer than it had been in days. "Being afraid doesn't change what has to be done."

"Some would run."

"You wouldn't." Mac Tíre studied the reins he held. "They are right about one thing. The Femorians are waiting for us."

"And?"

"And they will expect us to attempt breaching the castle using ladders, catapults, and battering rams." He glanced over at the group of archers. "If a small contingency sneaks past them and opens the gates from inside, we might stand a chance."

"What about Finn and Una?" I asked. "They could fly over the walls."

Una gasped.

I'd forgotten fairies could hear a flower petal fall to the ground from five miles away. Their gift kept them safe from prying humans who tried to sneak up on them. It also meant you couldn't keep secrets from fairies. They heard everything.

Una's wings were as pale as wisps of frosted breath. "Flying too close to the bonfires is suicide."

"These bonfires are enchanted," Liam explained. "You can tell by their color. They do more than burn. They are Goblin guards. They send out balls of fire as a warning to members of the Sidhe who fly too close. If someone like Una sustains a direct hit, her wings will burst into flames. She might not survive the fall."

"What about William?" I said. "He's not Sidhe. He's just under a spell. If we could reach him. . ."

"Technically, William is cursed," Síofra offered. "In any event, he's not a real dragon. He's under a spell so it would be even worse for him. The bonfires would not hesitate to burn him alive."

"Grace can use my wings," Síofra offered, slipping off her necklace.

****

One minute Síofra was holding the charm shaped like wings my mother had given her for her birthday and the next, Síofra had mumbled a few magic words, and the wings had grown as long as she was tall. Liam, Síofra and Finn discussed the best way to attach them using a harness and buckles, while Una shivered nearby, her wings so dark they blended into the shadows.

"You have to wear these wings," she said to me, her voice catching. "To control the wings a person needs more than voice commands, they need two good arms." She looked dejected. The worst I'd seen her since we'd begun our quest. "Plus, I cannot change into a giant until the next full moon. If I had a weapon…"

I squeezed Síofra's hand in silent support and understanding. When this was over—if we survived—I would teach Síofra how to use a sword.

Mac Tíre had his arms crossed over his chest and looked so upset I thought he might ignite. "Let me get this straight. Your plan is to strap wings on Grace and have her run a gauntlet through killer bonfires. All by herself. Are you all mad? I assume it's pointless to say I don't like this idea. Anyone bother to ask Grace her opinion?"

Liam said. "She'll be fine. There's a strong wind tonight. If she is high enough, she'll glide over the bonfires. You know how these wings operate. Take her to the roof of the tower ruins. The wind will do the rest."

Mac Tíre's voice was deadly calm. "Ah. You probably should tell her the wings are hard to control. Flying is not the issue. It's crash landing into the middle of the enemy's camp."

I couldn't take my eyes off Síofra. I didn't know what to do about the operation of the wings, but there was something I could do about a weapon. With Mac Tíre, Liam, and Finn engaged in a heated discussion, I snatched Finn's sword. It was the logical choice.

"Whoa," he said, moving toward me to grab it back.

Mac Tíre blocked his path.

"She took my sword."

Mac Tíre raised his eyebrow. "I'm sure she had a reason."

"Síofra needs a weapon," I explained, handing the sword to Síofra.

Mac Tíre smiled. "See. I told you."

With Finn brooding in the background I addressed another issue. "Couldn't help but overhear. Did someone say the wings were hard to control? Can't you cast a spell and make them more real? Like Una's."

Una said. "The more we enchant the wings the better chance the bonfires will detect the spell and attack. It's risky enough with you being…"

"Not now," Síofra interrupted. "Grace has enough to worry about."

"Like landing," Mac Tíre mumbled.

I frowned at him. "Not helping."

"Síofra," Mac Tíre said, "Tell her who gave you the wings."

Silence shredded the air as everyone concentrated

on Síofra. She held her arm against her chest and avoided my gaze. "Grace's mother gave you a pair of wings as well," she said.

"My mother gave Síofra a charm for her birthday," I said, defending my friend. I didn't understand why Mac Tíre was so upset. Then it sank in. "Mac Tíre. My mother gave you wings too?"

"I know what you're thinking Mac Tíre." Liam said. "But you can't use the wings. You're full Sidhe. Grace has better odds of flying over the bonfires undetected."

"Those are interesting choice of words, druid. I have a better idea. We all go. If we don't succeed, life won't be worth living."

Mac Tíre's comments sent off a new round of arguments. Una's wings were as dark as wet ash. She quivered like a leaf in a windstorm. Mac Tíre, Liam, and Finn were in a tight circle shouting over each other. Síofra kept glancing in the direction of the castle and Oghy U.

We all knew what was at stake. If we didn't defeat the Fire Lord or force him to reverse the spell by midnight, a short hour away, everyone under the spell would die. But it wasn't only their lives at risk as Mac Tíre had pointed out. Before the Book had been stolen, the Tuathans had reigned above and the Goblin Race below. As long as the Book of Invasions was missing we were all in danger, humans as well as magical beings. The balance of power had to be restored.

There were always times of unrest in the world when Goblins seemed to have the upper hand. But light always defeated the dark. If that changed…

The full moon shone ebony black against a blood-red sky. I wasn't sure I'd make it to the castle in time, but I had to try. I caught Síofra's glance and nodded. Without hesitation, she handed me the wings.

Chapter Twenty-Nine

An earsplitting scream tore through the night.

The Dobhar Chu's mate had found us.

While my friends distracted the monster, Mac Tíre and I headed toward the tower ruins in silence. Síofra had enlarged Mac Tíre's wings, and Liam and Finn had attached a harness. Mac Tíre was still not happy about my going but once I'd made up my mind he agreed to go along with my decision. I liked that he trusted me.

As we got closer to the tower, I remembered my mother had said the ruins belonged to a forgotten race. She'd actually used that term. Not O'Conner, O'Brien, or even Redmond, but *race*. My father wanted to tear it down. She forbade it.

The winding staircase was narrow, and the steps were uneven heights and widths. One side hugged the wall, the other was open. The construction was deliberate. It slowed the advance of an enemy and gave the tower occupants time to retreat or regroup. It was working. I had to concentrate or risk tripping and falling over the edge.

When we reached the roof, we had an unobstructed view of the valley. The roofline was higher off the ground than I'd first thought and it rose above the trees. Now was not the time to wonder if I was afraid of heights.

"Try not to look down," Mac Tíre said.

"I'll be flying. I have to look down." I said it as a jest to ease the tension and the rapid pounding in my chest. Mac Tíre wasn't smiling.

As serious as the plague, he helped me attach the wings to the harness, hefted the knapsack containing the Book over my shoulder, then set about fastening his. "This has to be the worst plan yet. You'll be a target. The Goblins believe you have the Book and will assume it's inside the knapsack."

"The Fire Lord will be suspicious if anyone else tries to return the Book," I reasoned. "According to Finn, he promised to release the sleeping spell only if I was the one who returned the Book."

"That's what bothers me. Why you? And why did he ask for you to return it, when John Dee stole it for the Goblins in the first place? None of this makes any sense." He rechecked my straps and stepped away. "Do three things. Land safely. Return the Book to its container. Hide."

"Would you settle for two out of three?"

"Not funny." Mac Tíre said. "The Fire Lord won't harm you as long as you have the Book. He cannot risk taking it by force. Enchanted objects, people and creatures all have complicated curses. Just ask your dragon friend, William."

Without meaning to, I glanced toward the night sky, half expecting William to appear. That he hadn't worried me. I brushed it aside. He probably had better things to do. I cleared my throat, voicing what had been on my mind most of the day. "I'm sure I can prove John Dee was lying when he said my mother helped him steal the Book."

Mac Tíre glanced toward the castle. "A few things

to remember before you fly. The wings will do all the work as your role is more of a captain. You tell them when, where, and at what speed you wish to land. Remember, they are enchanted wings and everything command is literal to them. Be sure you're specific. If you say stop, the wings will come to a screeching halt in midair and you'll plummet to the ground. If you order them to land they don't understand the difference between a safe landing and a crash landing. They survive either way."

I wrenched away. "You changed the subject. You can't believe John Dee."

"The Banshee said your mother stole the Tuatha's symbols of power."

"She's wrong," I snapped.

"Whoa. I'm on your side, Grace. Remember? According to Síofra, your mother was a frequent and welcomed visitor at the school. She had the perfect opportunity."

"You discussed this with Síofra?"

He took a ragged breath. "We can talk about it later."

"Later we could all be dead."

A muscle hardened along the side of his jaw. "You are not going to die."

"You can't know that."

The Dobhar Chu's mate roared below us. She'd broken through Finn's defense line.

****

The Dobhar Chu backed toward the tower entrance. Finn and his archers had the monster cornered. Unfortunately, the only exit open to her was the entrance to the tower.

226

"I'm not sure why she's hesitating," Mac Tíre said. "Once inside, she'll head straight for us. It is time for us to learn to fly." His expression turned so warm I felt I was standing too close to a roaring fire. "You are the reason we've come this far."

The tower vibrated. I suspected the Dobhar Chu's mate had made her decision, had plowed into the tower. Confirming my suspicions, below us was a sea of chaos. Finn ordered some of his men to follow her inside, while he and the others prepared to fly to the castle. I thought I saw Síofra duck into the tower but dismissed the notion. Naturally it started to rain.

Mac Tíre tilted his head toward the stairwell. "The Dobhar Chu's mate is inside the tower." He pulled me onto the ledge as his wings unfurled. "We have to leave." He soared above me. There was no fear in his dark eyes, only determination, and something else I couldn't quite identify.

Liam and Una along with Finn and his Sidhe archers had lifted in the air and were headed toward the bonfires, but Síofra was nowhere in sight.

Mac Tíre cupped his hands around his mouth and shouted. "The wings await your command."

"Fly," I shouted. Immediately, the wings unfurled and like the sails on a ship they caught the wind. I felt their need to soar free, to ride the currents of air as I lifted from the ledge and hovered. Then I gave the order to fly toward the castle.

In the next instant I shot straight into the sky then leveled out. Far below, the ring of fire glowed and pulsated with life. Wind and the sting of rain lashed against my skin. Numbing cold seeped into my bones. This was the best experience ever.

The bonfires grew a darker red as I drew near. I flew around the north tower and headed toward the south. "Prepare to land on the ocean side," I ordered. My hope was that the enemy knew we weren't attacking by ship, so the area wouldn't be as well guarded. Then I remembered Mac Tíre's warning and added, "Soft landing, please."

A fireball launched in my direction. I ordered the wings to dip and avoid the attack. The ball of fire sped past me and hit Una. She screamed and spiraled into the forest in a trail of smoke. A Sidhe warrior dove after her and I said a silent prayer he'd catch her in time.

Then the fireworks began in earnest. The air smelled of singed flesh and burning wings. Clouds of smoke made it difficult to navigate. I couldn't tell if I was still headed in the right direction. Screams of the wounded spiraled around me. One of the archers beside me took a direct hit. My heart raced. This was a bad idea. The cost was too high. Then I remembered all the people in the castle that were counting on me.

I remembered what Mac Tíre had said. I was the captain. I willed my rapid breathing to slow and let my instincts take over. I knew the direction of the castle. I could smell the sea and hear the crash of the waves. I dipped my wings and focused.

The smoke cleared the closer I came to the castle. Somehow Finn and the majority of his archers had made it through before me. Their bows ready, they let loose a volley of arrows even before they landed.

Out of nowhere I heard Mac Tíre. "We'll never make it. Head to Oghy U."

A fireball exploded in the air, singeing a corner of my wings. Mac Tíre tried to reach me, but flames shot out of a bonfire, separating us. My wings shuddered from the attack, rocking me back and forth. It took my full concentration to keep them extended. They seemed to want to curl together like an injured animal. They shuddered again, fighting my commands to keep going.

Another fireball whizzed past me. It was a miss. Pouring every ounce of energy into my voice, I shouted out the order to change course. This time the wings listened. In the blink of an eye, my speed increased. I banked to the left toward the school, aiming for a balcony that wrapped around three-quarters of the building.

I tilted downward into a nosedive. So much for soft landings.

Chapter Thirty

Moments before impact, my wings folded behind me like decorative fans used in the court of King Henry VIII. I wasn't as lucky. I spun one way, my knapsack the other. I landed hard and slid across the wood floor, slamming into the wall. The rough edges scraped across my side and doubled over in pain. My wound opened. Warm blood seeped through my bandages and it hurt to take a deep breath. It felt like I had cracked ribs.

And it was too quiet.

According to Finn, the school, like the castle, was under siege. Yet the only guard in sight stood at his post as ridged as a painted statue. At first, I thought he must be a human mercenary, like the Femorians hired as crew onboard their sky-ships. Looking closer, I recognized him as one of our castle guards.

Although asleep, he aimed his crossbow through narrow, loop-style slits in the wall. The openings were large enough to release arrows but positioned to give archers protection from attack. He looked like he had planned to release his arrows when he was frozen by the sleeping spell. But why was he here? In the past, even when we were under attack, Headmaster Mac Elatha refused our help.

Holding my side, I peered toward the opposite tower. Mac Tíre was fighting the Herding Boys. Liam, Finn, and the Sidhe archers had breached the castle walls and were in a desperate fight to take control. We were outnumbered. The Death Coach hovered above the castle like a vulture. Waiting. And I heard the Dobhar Chu roar.

The monster galloped toward the school, ducking and weaving as the bonfires sent balls of flames in her direction. That was odd. I wondered why the enchanted bonfires attacked one of their own until I saw Síofra. I had no idea how she'd tamed the Dobhar Chu, but there she was, riding the monster into battle as though they were the best of friends. I shouted to Síofra and waved my arm.

"I'm up here…"

"You're not dead. Pity."

I spun toward the familiar voice.

Gliding out of the shadows was my one-eyed Femorian tutor, or more precisely, Aillén, the Fire Lord. He looked exactly the same. One bloodshot eye in the center of his forehead, teeth filed to uneven points, breath like dead fish.

I pushed away from the wall and felt a sharp pain. I pressed my teeth together to swallow a groan. My knapsack laid a short distance away and in it the only weapon capable of killing him—Fionn mac Cumhaill's spear. The knapsack was too far away to grab without drawing attention. "You're not dead either."

"This is a second chance for us both."

"You can't win," I said, easing my hand over the hilt of my sword. "The Tuatha will defeat you, just like they did before."

His laugh heated the air. "The Tuatha are no better than the Irish warlords who fight amongst themselves or hide behind their fortresses rather than unite under one, true leader. When they learned the Book of Invasions had been stolen, they fled to the island of *Beg Ara* with their useless Red Branch champions, leaving children to fight their battles. We on the other hand, seized the opportunity." His laugh turned cruel. "If they stay too long, they become mortal. With luck they'll die of the Black Death, slow and painfully."

Stalling for time and keeping my back against the wall, I edged in the direction of the knapsack. It was more important than ever that we succeed. "Sailors from my father's ship claim to have seen *Beg Ara* while sailing around Ireland's west coast."

"And yet they refuse to believe we are real. Good for us and a fatal mistake for humans. Hand over the Book of Invasions."

"If I return it, will you release the spell and awaken everyone in the castle?"

Instead of answering, his eyes flicked toward the knapsack, confirming our suspicion that the ravens were spying on us. As quick as a snake, he slithered in its direction. We dove for the knapsack at the same time. He was faster.

He dumped out the contents. The herbs Mary had prepared for me spilled out first, exploding in a cloud of lavender mist. He shut his eye as though the herbs stung, while I snatched the spear and the Book. While he was distracted, I tucked the spear in my belt and the Book under my arm.

He covered his mouth and coughed. "What magic is this?"

Reminding myself to thank Mary if I survived, I scrambled out of his reach. I winced and took a shallow breath.

"Injured?" He sounded amused as his mouth curled in a sardonic grin. "Too bad it wasn't fatal. Now. Give. Me. The. Book."

I stood my ground and held out the spear. "I have a better idea. Reverse the sleeping spell and I won't use Fionn mac Cumhaill's weapon." The words held more confidence than I felt, because I wasn't sure if I could jam the spear into his mouth. The whole idea made my stomach churn. But even more, just because the Warrior Fionn mac Cumhaill had defeated Lord Aillén, that didn't mean I would succeed.

The Fire Lord pressed the empty knapsack into a ball, in the same way I knew he imagined crushing my skull. He blew on it until it burst into flames. It was Samhain Eve and Lord Aillén's fire powers were growing stronger. At midnight he'd be unstoppable.

I fought the impulse to run and hide, as Mac Tíre had advised.

Just when I thought my bluff hadn't worked, Lord Aillén flicked his wrist.

Instantly, the man standing guard awoke. He rubbed his eyes and yawned. When he saw me, he smiled. "Caught me napping, lass. Apologies. All seems quiet enough now, but earlier I thought I heard…" He shook his head and yawned again. "Does your mother know you're here? She insisted I guard the school." His expression froze when he glanced toward Lord Aillén. "Who are you?" The guard raised his crossbow, accurately assessing I was in danger. "Step back from Grace, or I'll be forced to kill you."

"Me first." The Fire Lord moved so fast he was a blur of smoke. He struck the guard with the back of his hand. Instead of looking statue-like as before, the guard crumpled to the ground.

The Fire Lord spun around and yanked the spear out of my grasp. "Never threaten an immortal." His words echoed the previous conversation between Mac Tíre, Síofra and me. He'd known all along we had the weapon. "I kept my part of the bargain. You keep yours."

"How do I know you won't kill everyone even after I give you the Book?"

"You don't." The expression in his eye filled with rage. He tossed the spear of Fionn mac Cumhaill aside as though it were a toy and from behind his back he drew a sword shaped like a crescent moon. "Before I'm finished, you will beg for death."

****

The Fire Lord lunged forward.

With the Book tucked under my arm, I ducked and rolled out of his reach. Mac Cumhaill's spear was on the far side where the Fire Lord had tossed it. I didn't know if that meant the spear wasn't a threat, or that's what the Fire Lord wanted me to believe. I fumbled with the wing's harness. Mac Tíre had strapped me into this contraption. He hadn't discussed how I'd get out. I tried to remember if he'd said anything about a release mechanism.

The Femorian moved so fast I didn't realize he was beside me until he grabbed me by the shoulders and flung me through the air as though I were as light as sea foam. I slammed against the wall so hard my teeth chattered. I shook my head, trying not to black out. I yanked on the buckles. They were stuck.

The Fire Lord wasn't wasting any time. He rushed over to me and threw me against the opposite wall. I felt like he was using me in some bizarre game where he bounced me off one wall and then the other. I held up my arms to ward him off, but he reached for my harness and threw me again.

The wings cracked under the impact. I slid down the wall. Pain no longer radiated from just my side. My whole body screamed in protest. I pushed my back against the wall and inched my way up.

The harness released. I thought about thanking him, but I doubted he'd appreciate the irony.

"Surrender!" he screamed. "You will never defeat us." His crazed voice seared through my thoughts. "The Goblins rise. Their brand of evil is an infectious disease. It seeks out the weak to use as its host and kills all who resist. And like a fatal disease, you never know you are infected until it is too late."

"You singled out the wrong family when you attacked the Logans," I said. "We never surrender. Especially to evil."

I'd forgotten how dramatic he was. And annoying. I drew Sea Pirate from its scabbard and wove it through the air in a figure eight, building its power. Ribbons of crimson light and molten silver trailed from the blade. The somber stone walls soaked in the glow, transforming the balcony. I felt that even without wings I could fly. Anything was possible.

Confidence drained from his expression. "You have the sword of *Foghlaí muir*. How is that possible? A girl has never possessed such a weapon. This changes everything." He cursed under his breath and pointed his sword toward the night sky.

His curved blade caught the reflection of the dark moon and shone like polished ebony. Winged creatures appeared silhouetted across the sky. As they descended, their wings pushed the heat of the bonfires closer.

"Red Dragons," I managed. Mac Tíre had been right to suspect them. They'd allied with the Goblins and were trying to help the Fire Lord escape.

"You're not going anywhere," I challenged. I raised my sword and attacked.

He blocked my blade with such force the impact vibrated through me, sending me across the floor. The sword quivered but held. I scrambled to my feet and rushed him.

The Red Dragons let loose a stream of fire, missing me by inches.

"Give up, Grace and I promise your death will be swift."

I widened my stance, holding out my sword. "I never give up."

He drew back his blade then froze.

A shadow crossed above us. William flew overhead and crashed into the lead Red Dragon. They spun in a death spiral as another shadow emerged.

The Selkie.

On the far side of the castle Mac Tíre had vanquished the Herding Boys. He leapt onto the railing of the balcony and motioned toward the ship. Connor was at the helm and Rowan on the riggings. Wind filled the ship's sails, as it banked toward Mac Tire, and dropped a rope ladder over its side. Mac Tíre scaled it and was on deck and in position behind the cannon in a manner of seconds.

"Impossible," the Fire Lord hissed. He'd observed the same thing I had. *The Selkie* might be small, but her crew were the bravest I'd ever seen, and Mac Tíre's reputation for never missing his target was legendary. I didn't have to see the Femorians to know they were running for cover.

High above, William was winning the battle with the Red Dragons. Those still remaining shrieked in defeat. The sound scorched the air as they banked to the south and disappeared into the clouds. Cannon fire blazed around us, exploding the sky with light. One blast punched a hole in the castle gate, another sent screaming Femorians over the walls.

Then the ship and its cannon turned toward us. I dove for cover in an alcove.

The Fire Lord wasn't as smart as he thought he was. Overly confident, he roared his defiance and shook his fist at the ship.

Mac Tire lit the fuse.

A direct hit.

The explosion threw the Fire Lord against the wall. He was singed, disoriented, but not dead. He was immortal and the only thing that could kill him was the spear of Fionn mac Cumhaill. But the explosion had weakened him, and I knew it would take a while for the Fire Lord to regain his full strength. Mac Tire had bought me some time.

While the Fire Lord was shaking off the attack, I scooped up the spear and shoved it into my belt, then held out my sword, Sea Pirate and waited.

It didn't take long.

The Fire Lord rose, swore something I can't repeat, and charged. We parried blow for blow. My strength grew as his faltered.

"You can't win," he shouted, but his words came between gulps of air as he glanced toward the castle. The Logan flag was restored and the castle under Finn's control.

"It is not over."

"I disagree." I raised Sea Pirate and with one blow, I knocked his sword out of his grasp.

The moon was near its zenith. The Fire Lord sucked in his breath and blew flames in my direction, but he was weak and his aim missed me.

He opened his mouth and drew in another desperate breath. Before he had a chance to attack, I withdrew the spear of Fionn mac Cumhaill from my belt and threw it into the Fire Lord's open mouth.

Chapter Thirty-One

The Fire Lord exploded into flaming ash.

A moment of relief washed over me. It wasn't over.

I secured the Book of Invasions and raced to find my mother.

Everywhere I looked, there was evidence the spell had been broken. People were waking up, confused, and disorientated. I couldn't stay to explain.

I raced to my mother's chamber in the castle. The Fire Lord's dying words replayed over and over in my thoughts like an ancient Gregorian chant. He'd said it wasn't over as though there were others coming for us. Even that was of secondary concern.

Cally had to be wrong. She'd said my mother was a thief and the Death Coach would bring her to the Land of the Dead for judgment.

When I reached my mother's room, the first indication something was wrong was that the tapestry hiding the entrance to the underground tunnels was ripped off the wall. The second was the state of my mother's rooms. A new fear shook me to my core. Was I too late?

The room had been torn to shreds. Tapestries were torn down. Large sections of stones and bricks were pulled out of the walls. Furniture lay broken and scattered. The green velvet coverings from her four-poster bed were ripped off and tossed into a corner.

Near a window, untouched by the chaos, my cat, Ella, perched on one of the first books my father had ever given me; *A Journey Beyond the Three Seas*. Beside it lay another touch of normalcy—my mother's charm bracelet.

A gold charm with a ruby stone commemorated the day she and my father were married and there was one in the image of a ship for the day I had been born.

I noticed ones I hadn't seen before. Miniature gold replicas of the Spear of Lugh, the Cauldron of the Goddess, the Sword of Nuada, and the Stone of Destiny, formed in the shape of a king's throne. I didn't like the direction of my thoughts.

Ella's eyes narrowed when she noticed me, but she didn't rush over as she normally would have, which made me even more nervous. She looked like she was standing guard.

Shaking away my foreboding, my voice trembled as I called out. "Mother! Where are you?"

A humming sound came from an area near a window overlooking the sea. She rose from behind rolled tapestries and scattered clothes, exposing a gaping hole in the wall.

She was alive. I gasped in relief and grabbed the door handle to steady my legs. "Mother…"

"There you are," she said, turning away. She wasn't talking to me. She was speaking to a bundle she cradled in her arms like a beloved child. Even from across the room, I recognized what it was. It was a pelt, a seal's pelt to be exact.

Chapter Thirty-Two

A chill chased over my skin as though a window had opened. I knew what it was with the same certainty I knew my own name. That scared me worse than Mouldywarps, Headless Horsemen, and Dobhar Chu combined.

"I've found you at last," she crooned, rocking the seal pelt in her arms.

Awareness as bright and sudden as a candle struck to light the secrets in the dark spread through me. Femorians hadn't ransacked the room, nor had some goblin from the Land of the Dead. My mother had.

Bits and pieces of things she'd said or done over the years started to fit together like the pieces of a puzzle. Hours she spent staring out to sea. Why she never ate meat, only fish. Why she was so protective of seals, forbidding anyone to harm them. I'd even caught her talking to them. Why she insisted I learn to swim…

"You're a Selkie." My voice trembled as I willed her to meet my gaze. She didn't seem to hear me. She kept singing to the bundle in her arms. I remembered the stories Mary had told me. Selkies sometimes took human form and bathed in the sun. Whoever captured them had to hide their pelts or they would return to the sea.

They were wonderful stories.

Magical.

Romantic.

And frightening because they were true.

Shivers ran over my arms, as though an icy winter breeze had entered the chamber. Father had claimed Mother hated the sea. He had said she refused to accompany him on his voyages. Or was that just a story he told, masking his real fear? He was afraid that the pull of the sea would be too great and that she would leave him, with or without her pelt.

Cautiously, I walked toward her, afraid if I moved too fast, she'd run away. I needed answers. If she were a Selkie that meant she was Sidhe. I swallowed, refusing to face that I shared her bloodline. I couldn't think about that now. Not yet.

The closer I drew to her, the more fearful I became.

She glanced over her shoulder, a gentle smile casting sunshine over her face. "Granuaile." She didn't sound surprised to see me.

She'd used the formal version of my name. In the past it had meant I was in trouble. Now it was something else entirely. It widened the gulf between us.

"There is so much to say and so little time," she said with a sigh. "I've wanted to tell you everything, but your father…well, he was afraid. Now it no longer matters. Were you aware that you share your father's thirst for adventure? The quest proves what I long suspected. But you also share my love and respect for the sea. You sense the turn of the tides, which direction the wind will blow, and the intensity of a storm, which is why you never get lost. It was wrong for your father to keep you from what you love, I realize that now. He feared losing you."

I knew she wasn't just talking about me. I moved

closer. "Mother, are you a Selkie?" I wanted her to deny it. Tell me I was foolish. Laugh like she used to when I was younger.

Her smile faded. "You look taller and wiser. Your quest accomplished more than I could have imagined."

How had she known about the quest? I rubbed my arms as my thoughts spun. "Father said you hated the water."

"I hate boats," my mother corrected. "They are too confining."

The emotional distance between us expanded. Had I ever really known her? Hot, angry tears welled in my eyes. It wasn't fair. I clenched my hands at my sides. How could she lie to me? Or think of leaving me?

I focused on reaching her, but she was so far away. Then I remembered what the Banshee had said about someone hunting her. "You will die if you return to the sea. The Banshee said your enemy is waiting for you. You must stay where it's safe."

My mother ignored what I'd said and reached for the bracelet, but Ella hissed and arched her back.

The cat meowed low, casting a look toward me as though caught between my mother and me. I had the strangest impression that Ella was trying to protect the bracelet.

"Ella. Move aside. I intend to bring the charms with me. You know I must." My mother knelt and motioned for Ella to come over to her. "I don't know what's got into Ella. Where was I? Oh, yes. If you are worried that someone is waiting for me that means me harm, do not fear. The Lord of the Sea failed before. I'm older now, and like you, wiser. I will be fine."

I was stunned. "Who are you talking about? Do

you know who is hunting you?"

Keeping an eye on Ella, she continued. "His name is Manannan Mac Lir. Before I met your father, the Lord of the Sea demanded I marry him. I didn't love him, but more than that, he already had a wife, several in fact. When I refused him, he threatened to have me killed. Gods are not used to being turned down. Anyway, I escaped and swam until I reached Clew Bay. Your father was near the shoreline, freeing a baby seal caught in a fisherman's net. I think he knew who I was the moment we met. Because of his kindness to the seal, I allowed him to view me in my human form. He asked me to marry him." A faraway smile lit her face from within.

My mother smoothed her hand over the bundle of smooth, ebony fur she held. Her smile grew in warmth, as though she'd walked into a ray of sunshine. "When you were born, I asked your father to hide my pelt. I didn't want to risk the temptation."

Cautiously, I edged closer, afraid to startle her. "What changed?"

"I had the strangest dreams while you were gone. While I slept I dreamed someone whispered my pelt's location. When I awoke I knew it was behind one of the tapestries. I thought I could resist, but the pull of the sea is too powerful."

"It's a trap. Someone wanted you to find it. Please don't leave me."

My mother's expression drifted away again, as though reliving her past. "I hear Manannan's voice on the wind. Sometimes it's soothing, saying all is forgiven. Most of the time, however, he's angry, conjuring waves to lash at my feet while I walk along the shore. I thought he'd forgotten me after all these years."

Her eyes narrowed in the same way as Ella's had moments before. In the next, she'd snatched the charm bracelet from the cat and slipped it on. Ella looked as surprised as I felt. I'd barely seen Mother move.

****

The charms on my mother's bracelet chimed and caught the light. They turned fire-gold, highlighting the inlaid enamels of green, red, and black, an innocent piece of jewelry with hidden secrets. Síofra's charm was an enchanted set of wings. I doubted the four Tuathan symbols my mother wore were mere representations.

"Did you help John Dee steal the Book?" I accused, knowing my voice was laced with anger, disappointment and hurt.

"Of course not," she responded calmly. "By the time I discovered it was missing, it was already too late."

"How does John Dee fit into all this?

"A pawn, perhaps, but it is too early to tell. At first, I thought Balor of the Evil Eye or the Lord of the Dead, Crom Dubh was behind the theft, but now I'm not so sure. That's why I must go. My leaving will keep you safe. I thought sending you on a quest would be enough. You were in grave danger if you stayed behind."

I didn't know what she was talking about. "Mother, I was attacked by Goblins. If it weren't for my friends, I'd be monster food. You didn't send me. I volunteered."

Mother shook her head sadly. "I know you better

than you know yourself. You have great courage, loyalty and a sense of duty that few possess. The castle and all you loved were in jeopardy. It is not in your nature to stand on the sidelines while others risk their lives."

"My tutor was the Fire Lord. He almost killed me."

"I never suspected the Goblins would go so far. Sending the Fire Lord told me how desperate they'd become. I'm still not sure why they believe you are a threat." Her voice trailed off as she fingered one of the gold charms that looked like a replica of the Cauldron of the Goddess.

And then it all became clear.

"Mother, you and Síofra have the power to shrink or enlarge objects. You stole the symbols of the Tuatha de Danaan, which they say is their source of power. No wonder they want them back. Mac Tíre was right."

"He usually is."

"You have to return them."

"Impossible. They will keep me safe long enough to help me discover who is behind the Goblin rising." Her voice was deeper, more lyrical, like the currents in the ocean. "You must tell no one I have them."

I shook my head, trying to take it all in. "You stole the Tuathan symbols which are their source of power," I repeated. "There will be consequences."

I almost crossed the physical distance that separated us, but it only brought me more pain. She'd changed. Her skin was darker and her eyes wider. She reminded me of Connor and Ronan.

"If I figured out that you can shrink them in size, so will the Femorians. You're not safe," I added, trying to reason with her.

My mother turned toward the window.

"Stop," I shouted. "The Banshee warned me that the Death Coach has come for you. I have a sky-ship. We could escape."

"I don't expect you to understand," she said in a faraway voice I barely recognized.

She wasn't thinking clearly. Mary said that happened when a Selkie came in contact with their pelt. All they could think about was the ocean. I had to stop her.

I grabbed for the pelt.

She was faster.

My mother snatched it out of my grasp in a blur of speed. She raised her hand and a wave of power shoved me across the room. I hit the wall with the realization that my gentle mother had super strength. The thought collided with awareness that there was another side of her. A darker side.

When I tried to stand, my legs felt like boiled kelp.

She swept the pelt around her shoulders and climbed onto the windowsill. Waves crashed below. She tilted her head as though she'd heard them call her name. The realization chilled me to the bone. My mother smiled, but I barely recognized the expression as belonging to my mother. She looked happy.

"They will kill you," I said.

"Do not worry about me, Granuaile. They will have to catch me first."

Chapter Thirty-Three

Only hours had past, but it felt like a life-time as I ventured outside into the thick of the festival for Samhain Eve and my birthday. I had reverently replaced the Book of Invasion in its secret alcove at Oghy U., and so far, things seemed back to normal. Except they weren't. My parents were missing.

The last words my mother had spoken to me before she disappeared into the foaming sea haunted me still *"They will have to catch me first."*

Bonfires blazed higher and higher as though competing to see who could touch the heavens first. No longer enchanted, their glow was warm and welcoming. People danced around the fires wearing masks that resembled animals of the forest. Still others played the fiddle, or flute, or clapped their hands together in time to the music.

Superstitions died hard in Ireland even though the village priest had blessed us and assured everyone that his prayers would keep the demons and ghosts away. No one mentioned the time they were asleep as though they wanted to pretend it was a dream. Instead, they built the fires higher, carved out more pumpkins, and donned costumes.

The representatives of the O'Brien clan had appeared a few hours ago and we'd scrambled to make them comfortable in the castle. In all that had happened, we'd forgotten they were invited in the first place. I'd avoided talking to the chieftain's son and I'd heard he believed it was because I was shy. None of that seemed important after all we'd been through.

The clouds still cloaked the night sky, but the winds had died down and the seas were calm. At least my mother wouldn't be out in a storm, I rationalized, as I tried to give the reality that she was a Selkie a positive spin.

It wasn't working. It reminded me that the Lord of the Sea and the Dullahan were hunting her and that she and I shared the same bloodline. I held out my hand, trying to gauge if the webbing between my fingers was more pronounced. Would I turn into a seal when I got older? I didn't even like eating fish that much. And then of course there was the fact that my father and his crew were still prisoners of the Goblins.

Tension crackled through me like sparks in the flames. I felt like I was treading water and I didn't like the feeling.

Students from Oghy U., families from the surrounding villages, and castle inhabitants danced in circles in the same way the druids had in centuries past. Paddy twirled Mary until they both were breathless. Laughing, they beckoned me to join them. When I shook my head, they danced past me, blurring with the other dancers in a sea of amber, green and gold.

A flock of children from the nearby village raced past me chasing what their parents called fireflies, but what I knew were fairies who'd come to join in the celebrations.

No one mentioned my parents' disappearance, not even Mary. If anyone spoke of them, it was to say that they were late and would arrive soon. I knew differently.

I stood on the perimeter of the celebrations. The noise pushed against me until I felt crushed by its weight. We shouldn't be celebrating. We should prepare for battle. I knew with every fiber of my being that the Femorians hadn't given up.

I twisted the ring my mother had given me on my finger as though that might help bring it all into focus. If I told Liam or Finn that my mother had stolen the four symbols of the Tuatha, I could let them handle it. I could walk away.

The thought made me feel worse.

I'd accomplished my quest. The sleeping spell was vanquished, and the Book of Invasions returned. No one would blame me if I settled back into my old life at the castle as though everything was right with the world.

The noise of the celebrations pressed in around me again. The singing roared in my ears, making my head throb.

The chieftain's son came up beside me, tall and lean, like a young birch tree and dressed in his finest. He motioned to the crowd of dancers. "My father and I appreciate that you organized a celebration in our honor."

A week ago, I might have nodded and ignored his misunderstanding. I was no longer that person. I kept my gaze focused on the bonfires feeling their strength merge with mine. "The celebrations for the festival of Samhain Eve were planned long before you were invited, but I'm glad you like them."

He slowly turned toward the bonfires and frowned.

"We weren't aware the Logans still celebrated All Hallows Eve. Aren't you afraid you'll wake the Walking Dead?"

"Not anymore." I *really* wanted to tell him it already had happened, but he looked like he was about to jump out of his skin as it was.

He arched an eyebrow and gave me the once over as though seeing me for the first time. "Why are you dressed like a man?"

I rested my hand on the hilt of Sea Pirate. "Queen Maeve, one of Ireland's greatest warriors, dressed as I do, and she was not thought the less for it. It is my honor to protect my family and home."

Those same thin eyebrows drew together. "I meant no disrespect, but there is no need for you to risk your life to protect the castle. My father and I are here to take care of you." The corner of his mouth turned up in a lopsided grin. "Would you care to dance? I learned that today is your birthday."

"She dances with me." Mac Tíre smiled and held out his hand toward me. His voice was calm and soothing like waves lapping over the shore, but like the ocean, his voice was laced with warning directed toward the chieftain's son.

Ignoring the chieftain's son's scowl, I joined Mac Tíre in the dance circle. When Mac Tíre turned toward me, his expression caught me off guard. His smile was infectious and as though by magic he chased away my dark mood. I'd only known him a week, yet it felt like we'd been friends all our lives. I slipped my hand into his and laughed as he spun me into the circle of dancers. I didn't have to wear a mask, like the villagers. I could be myself with Mac Tíre.

"Who is that guy?" he said.

"The person my parents wanted me to marry," I said, raising my voice over the music and laughter. "The marriage between our clans would increase Logan's land holdings and make them a powerful force in this part of Ireland."

His laughter was so abrupt it caused those around us to turn and smile. "The Logan clan is already a formidable force on land and sea. I've only known you a short time, and I've learned that you have the strength, courage, and intelligence to increase the power and reputation of the Logans on your own, with or without a husband."

I wanted to believe him. But why was it that people could see the strength in us before we see it in ourselves?

The lively tunes of fiddles and bagpipes swirled around me, raising the tempo of my pulse and blocking out my thoughts. Mac Tíre's hand was warm and although no one in the circle held hands, he hadn't let go of mine.

He also hadn't mentioned my mother's disappearance, or that she was a Selkie. Plus, and this was a big one, he hadn't said any "I told you so's" when he had learned she had stolen the symbols that were the source of the Tuathan's power. Mother had told me not to tell anyone. But my friends were the only ones I could trust, not telling them felt like a betrayal after all we'd been through together.

"Will you marry him?" Mac Tíre asked.

"I don't know," I answered honestly.

A line of dancers separated us, sweeping me in one direction and Mac Tíre in the other. The tempo increased. Faces blurred and I felt lost again. My parents had arranged my marriage, and it occurred to me that I didn't know the chieftain's son's name. With my parents gone, was I still obligated to fulfill their wishes, or could I refuse? And was Mac Tíre right? Could I increase my family's wealth and influence on my own?

Mac Tíre had appeared again, reached for my hand and pulled me closer. "Can we go someplace and talk?" He glanced toward the night sky. The Death Coach made a pass across the full moon, as though waiting. "I have a little time before I leave."

I wasn't sure what he was talking about. "Where are you going?"

He didn't answer.

Hand in hand, we raced away from the dancers toward a grove of oak trees and ducked under a canopy of branches. When we stopped he turned me toward him and held both my hands in his.

His gaze was intense. No longer calm, his voice reminded me of rolling thunder. "Wait for me." He lifted my hand, kissed it, and then placed the golden pendant and chain that had belonged to his mother in the palm of my hand. "I want to give you a birthday present." He paused. "Forget I asked you to wait for me. I had no right. You have a life here and responsibilities."

He started to pull away, but I held onto his hand and wouldn't let go. "Don't leave."

Bonfires blazed higher, spreading their warmth to the corners of the festival grounds. I lifted my gaze, holding my breath as he leaned down and brushed his lips against mine. It was a feather's touch that for a moment chased away the fear.

My first kiss.

Then he turned and disappeared into the crowd, taking the warmth with him. He hadn't told me where he was going.

I called out his name over the deafening sounds of laugher and music, then shoved past the dancers and headed toward a small rise overlooking the celebrations to get a better view. The crush of people made it impossible to distinguish one person from the next.

Síofra appeared beside me. It no longer bothered me that she could appear and disappear without warning. It wasn't that I was used to it so much as that I understood. Like how a cat moved soundlessly or when a leaf fell. You didn't analyze it. You just knew that it was part of their nature.

"Nice job taming the Dobhar Chu's mate," I said, rising on my tiptoes to see if I could find Mac Tíre over the tight circle of dancers.

"The Dobhar Chu's mate's name is Baibin," Síofra's voice sounded strained, distracted. "She came here to thank us for riding the countryside of her husband's control and wanted to offer us her help if we ever needed her." Síofra put her arm around my shoulders. "I know you don't want to talk about Baibin." Síofra paused. "The Death Coach disappeared."

It felt as though my heart had stopped beating. "That doesn't mean it found my mother. It could have taken the souls of any of those who lost their lives when we secured the castle, even the Fire Lord's."

"It's possible."

I took in a deep breath. Síofra's tone of voice

wasn't convincing. "Do you think Mac Tíre followed the Death Coach?"

"That is also possible. I overheard he, Connor and Ronan discussing that they believed the Death Coach might lead them to where the Goblins are holding your father and his crew."

Her news rocked me off center as though I was standing on a ship battered by gale-force winds.

"They plan to launch a rescue? Why didn't he tell me?"

From the far side of the festival, the chieftain's son was weaving his way through the dancers in my direction. I fingered the golden pendant and chain Mac Tire had given me and slipped it around my neck. "Mac Tire said I should forget him. That I have responsibilities on Clew Bay."

Síofra looped her arm through mine. "That sounds like him and he's right. You've done enough. You can take the ring off and concentrate on your human side." She hesitated. "The chieftain's son looks nice. I don't think your parents would choose someone for you who was hideous."

I smiled at her attempt at humor, hoping she was right. "You changed the subject, but I won't deny who I am. I can't sit still while my family and friends are in danger. That is not who I am. My mother hid who she was, and it almost destroyed her. It still might."

"She loved you and thought she was doing the right thing when she hid the truth from you."

I took in a shallow breath. "I wished my mother had trusted me."

Mary and Paddy had delayed the chieftain's son and engaged him in conversation as though they knew I needed more time to think about what I wanted to do next. Mary denied she could read a person's thoughts, but she always seemed to know mine. Like the night we couldn't find my cat, Ella. Mary knew I'd search for Ella, despite my parents' objections and was waiting for me at the door leading outside with a torch to light my way and a treat for Ella.

The chieftain's son backed away from Mary and Paddy and headed toward me. Patrick looked nice, but could you judge character from a person's appearance?

I drew myself up to my full height, thinking how useful it would be if I could transform into a giant like Síofra. There were times when that would come in handy.

He reached my side and made a slight bow. "It occurs to me," he said holding out his hand toward me, "that we haven't been formally introduced. My name is Patrick. After talking to Mary and Paddy, it also occurred to me that because of your parents' death, you'd need time to grieve. I'd like to put your mind at ease. Instead of us marrying this winter, spring is soon enough. May I have the next dance?"

His speech was an emotional check list. Introduce yourself. Check. Pretend empathy. Check. Set the wedding date. Check. Check. I glanced toward the hand he'd outstretched toward me. It was callused, a swordsman's hand. There was a time when that would have been enough. Not anymore.

"My parents are not dead."

He reached for my hand. "I have lost those I loved as well. Your parents live on in you."

I yanked my hand free. Anger and frustration bubbling to the surface. "They aren't dead, and I don't care if you believe me. I'm going to find them and the friends who left to rescue them."

His smile slipped, and he drew back, eyes darkening like the shadows around us. "You are more than I expected, Grace Logan. We will find them together."

A word about the author...

Pam Binder is an award-winning Amazon and New York Times Bestselling author who loves Irish and Scottish myths and legends. She writes historical fiction, contemporary fiction, time travel, young adult, and fantasy.

Pam is a conference speaker and teaches two year-long novel writing courses, After The First Draft and Write Your Story.

http://pambinder.com

Thank you for purchasing
this publication of The Wild Rose Press, Inc.

For questions or more information
contact us at
info@thewildrosepress.com.

The Wild Rose Press, Inc.
www.thewildrosepress.com

To visit with authors of
The Wild Rose Press, Inc.
join our yahoo loop at
http://groups.yahoo.com/group/thewildrosepress/